Also by Bette Howland

W - 3

BLUE IN CHICAGO

THINGS

TO

COME

AND

GO

Bette Howland

THINGS
TO
COME
AND
GO

Three Stories

Alfred A. Knopf   New York   1983

5/1983
gen'l

The author wishes to express her gratitude to the MacDowell Colony and the Ragdale Foundation for their warm hospitality.

THIS IS A BORZOI BOOK
PUBLISHED BY ALFRED A. KNOPF, INC.

"The Life You Gave Me" originally
appeared in *Commentary*.

Library of Congress Cataloging
in Publication Data
Howland, Bette.
Things to come and go.
I. Title.
PS3558.O927T5 1983
813'.54   82-48724
ISBN O-394-53032-2

Manufactured in the
United States of America
First Edition

THINGS
TO
COME
AND
GO

BIRDS
OF
A
FEATHER

My father's family look alike; they all take after their mother's side. Abarbanel was her maiden name, and that's what my mother calls them to this day —"the big brassy yak-yakking Abarbanels." They have a creaturely resemblance. Large swarthy virilely pock-marked men; beard-blued cheeks, Persian hair, palpable noses. (That goes for Aunt Honey too; I guess that's why she never married.) My grandfather must have wondered what he was doing in their midst. I know I did. Not in so many words; but even a child could see that the old man was not of the same make; and at our long noisy family dinners—all talking at once, shouting over the rest, getting louder and louder, like people carrying on in a foreign language—he used to fall asleep at the table; his head laid to the wine-stained cloth, his two hands under his cheek.

Not a bristle stirred in his mustache.

I would be lying if I said I remembered him well, but that much for sure; he had a mustache. A bundle of yellow straw on his lip. A bale; a broom. It tickled and scratched, it *nibbled* my cheek. What a fuss I put up when I had to kiss him, turning my face this way and that. His brows were of the same coarse stuff, but white, and so thick his eyes just glimmered.

For the rest, I seem to recall someone slight and stooping, his baldness patched by a satin skullcap. He never had much to say for himself. Except when he sneezed. Then he got violent:

Got-choo! Got-you!

That was a surprise. So he sneezed in English. I kept waiting for him to say something more; something else that I could understand. But he never did.

My grandfather's name—our family name—was one of those Russian mouthfuls; you'd probably have a hard time pronouncing it, anyhow. In the old country (that would be Odessa, on the Black Sea; I thought of it as really black, rolling black, like Honey's eyes) he had carried on the family trade—the manufacture of paint, putty, and varnish. Whatever it was they put in the stuff in those days, it sure must have been strong; the tips of his fingers were pink and shiny. Not that anyone knew or cared, until one time when he had to make application for some kind of license. Then lo and behold: my grandfather had no fingerprints.

This was Chicago, as I should have mentioned by now; and what's more, Prohibition. So you know what that means. Mobsters. Machine guns. Rat-a-tat-tat. The cops (I suppose it was; this happened long before I was born) decided to have some fun with him; teasing the old man, threatening to lock him up and throw away the key. The nerve of these greenhorns! Coming over here without their fingerprints. They had him believing he had done something wrong, broken the law—a hoodlum, a gangster, worse than Al Capone. Guilty of the crime of No Fingerprints.

He was scared they were going to send him back where he came from.

My grandfather had had another family there. That first wife went off her head during a pogrom, smothered the children and herself. A son survived. The old man left him behind when he came to America—because what was a widower to do, with a small child on his hands?—meaning to send for the boy when he got settled. But other things happened instead; they lost touch. No one else in the family ever so much as laid eyes on this eldest son, their own half brother, until a couple of years after the war. Aunt Flor's husband (that was the second one, the one they say made a killing on the black market) pulled some strings and brought him over. And by then the old man was dead.

Sometimes, when I had been put to bed on a heap of rough coats, listening to those voices at the table—still going at it (only I could never make out what the shouting was all about, or if the loudness was anger or laughter)—I would wake up in Honey's room. What wonderful things could happen! So I had been carried off in my sleep, and didn't even know it.

There would be the full-blown cabbage-rose wallpaper; the high white bed; the sheer curtains surging at the windows—the light itself battering its way in; and Honey's large underwear all over the quilt and posts. Slips, stockings, bloomers, brassieres; puffed and puckered, as if with her flesh.

And there, right next to me, on a pile of pillows, would be Honey's head, her smudge-black hair. Her great big nose, in profile; her trimmed eyelid; the twirl of a spit curl taped to her cheek.

I had to blink; so surprised I could hear my own eyes pop open.

And with that, quick as a wink, Honey would roll one gleaming globe of an eye at me, grinning at me sidewise and making a clicking noise in her cheek.

All the Abarbanels were cheek-clickers and cheek-pinchers. But Honey mostly clicked. I could see the hidden gold in her teeth.

Hiya, kiddo. (That was the way she talked.) How's my little bright-eyes, huh? My besty little Esti? (That was my name.) Tee Gee. Another beautiful day. (Honey never spoke the name of the Lord; she used initials.)

As if she was the one who had waked up first; as if the whole time she had been dying for me to wake up too, lying in wait, only pretending to be asleep—I thought grownups only pretended to sleep—just so she could spring her surprise on me. She put her legs over the side of the bed, and the springs rose with her.

I must have been a sourpuss. That's what I think. People were forever teasing me, making faces, popping eyes and poking out chins. It was a long time before I caught on; they were imitating *me* staring at *them.*

On the dressing table with the tipping mirror I sniffed her powder boxes and cold-cream jars and little blue bottles of Evening in Paris; they came from the dime store. That's what everyone gave Honey for presents, the same way they gave me puzzles and games. When I got old enough to save money, that's what I got for her too. She showed me a pin in the shape of a battleship, set with white beads, and held it up so the light could shine through. It read (she said): Remember Pearl Harbor.

.   .   .

An upright piano stood in the dining room, and a bench so stuffed with sheet music you had to sit on it to shut it. When the sisters, Honey and Flor, sidled up—side by side—it shut. You bet. Flor played; Honey turned the pages. They sang Yiddish songs in quavering voices, and they sang The Latest; their shoulders rocking, Flor pumping pedals.

Flor was big, like all the Abarbanels, but her skin was smooth and dead white—scalp white—white as the part that drove up the middle of her wiry black hair. Her brows grew together over her nose; it plunged between them, straight to the hilt, her eyes on either side wide and divided.

Hard red nails clacked the keys.

> *O the stars* at *night*
> Are *big* and *bright*
> (Clap clap clap clap)
> *Deep* in the *heaaart* of *Texxx-asss*
>
> O the *prai-ree moon*
> Is *like per-fume*
> (Clap clap clap clap)
> *Deep* in the *heart* of *Tex-as.*

Honey cracked her gum; she flashed her fillings. Her eyes flashed too. And something in the way she tossed her head, slapping the music sheets—something rich in her throat and keen in her glance—made me fear she was fighting back tears.

. . .

My father had a falling out with the rest of his family, and we didn't go to that house anymore. Flor's husband —that was the first one, the dentist; he was away in the war—had set up an office at the front of the flat. The padded chair, the drooling sink, the name in decal letters backwards on the window; all was gloomy with preservation. And the living room as well; Venetian blinds drawn to keep carpets from fading; bedsheets protecting sofas and chairs; knickknacks on shelves safe behind glass. A pair of large dolls sat propped on cushions, in dusty velvet dresses and brittle nests of wigs: doll-lashes rigid, doll-gazes unblinking.

Once, when my mother was dragging me along, shopping on Twelfth Street, she gave my arm a yank; we stopped short. She had seen them coming. —The mother, the two daughters, their pocketbooks over their arms. The old woman—my grandmother—had all the Abarbanel characteristics in their original, proudest, most forceful form. The coarse powerful nose; the forbidding scrolls of the nostrils; two great slabs of breasts slung to her belt. Their slope was formidable. All her authority seemed vested in them.

Her head had turned iron gray, but her brows and her moles were still black-haired.

They looked at us and we looked at them and then my grandmother nudged Flor on one side of her, and Honey on the other, and all three turned right about— arms linking, purses swinging. If you think there was a family resemblance from the front, I wish you could have seen them, just then, from the back. You couldn't tell them apart. The three sets of hips bolstered their skirts like the sofas under the bedsheets. I wondered if they were lifting and sticking out their behinds at us.

What makes you think they weren't? my mother said. I wouldn't put it past them. What else can you expect? From a bunch of Abarbanels?

All this time, my grandfather had never stopped coming to our house. He was a house painter; my father often helped him out. I liked to watch them slicing up curly strips of wallpaper, smoothing on clear sweet-smelling paste. (It tasted sweet too.) I don't need to tell you what the brushes reminded me of. The old man had never talked before and he didn't start now; but there he would be, in our kitchen, elbows on the table, stirring his tea with a long tinkling spoon. Lemon swirled in the glass; yellow motes; sedimented sunlight. He smoked the cigarettes he rolled for himself with a flick and a lick—it was the tobacco that made his mustache straw color—the twisted ends lighting up in a blaze.

I was sure his mustache was going to catch fire, go up in smoke. Maybe it didn't; but his eyebrows did.

One day I happened to look up and see Uncle Reuben standing on our front porch, putting something into the mailbox. It was summer; the screen was on the hook. I went and peered out.

Reuben was the baby of the family; he had just been called up for the Army. He was in uniform. Under the button flaps of his cardboard khaki shirt pockets he had something like breasts, and his face was still lumpy and purplish with acne.

He brought it close and spoke through the screen.

Tell my brother Sammy his father died, will you? Reuben said—and turned and ran down the stairs. They sounded as if he was trampling on them.

At the bottom he stopped and looked back.

Esti? Hey, Esti?

He waited. I kept looking. He shook his head.

Aw, forget it, Reuben said.

The raised lid of the box was padded in puffy glazed satin, like the tops on boxes of Valentine candy, and a red velvet rope stretched in front of it. People moved past, looking in. My mother held me up to see what they were looking at. Right away—even before I knew—the way you snatch your hand from scalding water before you know you got burned—tears struck; bulged from my eyes.

Through their spangled glitter I saw the white eyebrows, the yellow mustache, the hooked nose between. The two dark flues. All, all, seemed stiffened—dried—made of straw, like his mustache. And worse yet—I knew nobody would believe me if I tried to tell—his wrinkled cheeks looked *rouged. Powdered* too. Even the hairs in his nostrils. Powdered!

How many times had I been held up like this, for the old man's kiss; and cried, and turned my face away, and seen—from the glimmer—that I must be hurting him. Now he had turned his face from me. Once and for all: a cold rebuff.

Each hair stood out—by itself—shrivelled and still.

My Uncle Reuben lives in Lungo, southeast of Chicago, over the Indiana line; rounding the curved bottom of Lake Michigan. There are expressways now; but in the early fifties, when Reuben first moved there, it used to take forever driving past the refineries and mill towns. Hammond, Whiting, East Chicago. "Roll up your windows, everybody. We're in Gary!" Sometimes the storage tanks and smokestacks looked like organ pipes, and sometimes they looked like plumbing. I can taste the air just thinking about it.

Lungo had been planned as a model community, laid out to the last detail—even the names of the streets. (Alice, Betty, Carol, Diane . . .) The buildings were to have been Mediterranean—I think it was Mediterranean—red tile and pink stucco. The train station, long boarded up; the one store in town that stayed open all year (PackageLiquorBeer, read the vertical sign); the hotel on the water that kept changing hands. —New owners slapped another coat of paint on the turquoise swimming pool.

Along came the Depression, and that was that; not much else ever got built. In the woods, bent rusted street signs and cracked sidewalks might pop up in the middle of nowhere; a snake squirting across cement, parting the grass. Lungo himself had gone broke and ended up in jail.

In the postwar boom, the land was bought up by

another developer. Small tract houses, yellow brick, lots of gravel and sodded grass. From Route 101, the old Red Arrow Highway, you saw all roofs and no trees. Aunt Flor's husband—I'm talking about the second one now; Boaz Benjamin by name—had an interest in the construction company, and Reuben got a deal on the house when he got married. The summer after, I stayed with Reuben and his wife because she was big and pregnant with the twins—a boy and a girl. "You name it, I got it," Reuben said, passing out cigars. Now I was back for another summer as a mother's helper. My parents had gone to California; my father had been laid off and was looking for work. And Reuben's wife thought she might be expecting again.

Her name was Luellen, and you weren't to call her Lou. That was a *boy's* name. That fat lazy good-for-nothing red-headed hillbilly, Reuben called her. (The twins, black-haired as Reuben, fair-skinned as Luellen, he called *jewbillies.*) "I ain't fat neither," Luellen would say, turning out her lip. And she wasn't; not by Abarbanel standards. She was soft and white—pearly white—convex and lucent as those beads on Honey's long-forgotten pin. Her eyes were chips of blue fused glass; and her long red hair was smooth and supple as a skein of silk.

From the front she seemed to have "hardly no nose at all." But from the side, there it was—embedded in her face like a spigot.

The living-room walls were practically glass; photos of the twins, all the same pose—two identical pairs of eyes, two wispy topknots caught in ribbon. Luellen had signed a contract with a photography studio in Michigan City to take one framed full-color portrait and six wallet-sized snaps, each and every month, for five years. The salesman had told her she was getting two for the price of one.

Reuben hit the ceiling. "Two for the price of one means the twins, dope."

Then there were the encyclopedias, also a pair—Jr. and Sr.—each with its own wood-stained laminated bookcase. Reuben hadn't unpacked any boxes yet; he was still hoping to send it all back. The salesman had told Luellen that the books would be paid for by the time the children were old enough to read them.

"Oh yeah?" Reuben said. "Whose kids? Mine or theirs? That's all I wanna know."

All through the house, it was the same story; two of this and two of that; toys, buggies, strollers, cribs, often with the price tags on them. Even twin playpens.

That time the salesman sat beside Luellen on the couch, turning pages, a photo album open on his knees. He was tall and thin and all doubled up, like Donny's jackknife. (Donny was my boyfriend; I'll get to him in a minute.) Babies in bandages. Babies in casts. Babies in slings. Eyes wide open in hospital cribs. They had fallen out of playpens sold by rival manufacturers; playpens which failed to meet the strictest scientific standards.

All of a sudden the salesman clapped his book shut and jumped up. His arms and his jacket flapped at his sides.

"No, lady, no. It's no use," he said. "I ain't gonna show you no more. I can see you got a soft heart. I hate to show pitchers like this to a susceptible individule like yourself. So don't ask me."

Luellen was wearing pedal pushers (we called them toreador pants), scuffed ballet slippers, and a nylon sweater so thin her bra showed right through; shiny cones, cornucopias. Her breasts rolled over the tops. She was all rolls, curves, funnels of flesh—her cheeks, her chin, her lip. It was slowly spreading. (Her teeth were bad and she hid them when she smiled.)

The pink of her lipstick—a shade called Blazing Kiss —gave her nose a pink gloss too.

"All right, all right. If you insist," the salesman said, dragging a crumpled length from his pocket. A handkerchief. Luellen bunched it gamely in her fist. "But you gotta promise me now; you're not gonna cry."

He folded himself up again, his order form on his knee, and unscrewed the cap from his fountain pen. "You know what? I been thinking. With twins and all? You might be safer off with *two?*"

Reuben tried to get the check stopped, but it had been cashed on the spot. That did it; he put his foot down. —Took Luellen's name off the checking account; called the stores and warned them no more credit; placed an ad in the classifieds: *I will no longer be responsible for any debts other than my own.* (I had often wondered what made people take out ads like that.) And, as a parting shot and just to make sure, he forbade Luellen to answer the phone or the door. Tante Malkeh or I (Tante Malkeh was the old Abarbanel aunt who had come to live with them) had to go and see first if it might be a salesman.

That was fine with Luellen; she never liked to answer anything, anyway.

What she liked was lying on the bed with her feet propped up—ten stubby frosty-pink toenails—smoking and reading confession magazines. A fan stood beside her on the chair, moving its wire muzzle from side to side. The breeze lifted the covers and rattled the slick pages. In her eagerness, she licked her forefinger as she turned them; lapping them up.

There was a whole stack of magazines under the bed.

"You c'n always read-em again," Luellen said. "Once you forget what's in-em."

Luellen was from a river valley; the banks overflowed six springtimes out of seven. She was full of tales of the "heartships" of farm life and the floods. Her accent got harder; the twanging and snapping of strings breaking on a banjo. Her lipstick-stained cigarette bobbed away in her mouth: the ruby-red lips of the drowning Clementine.

"One morning Gran-daddy, he hops outta bed, and finds hisself standing in two feet a water. Up to his knees. His nightshirt is dripping. And the bedroom—get this—is on the secont floor.

"That ain't nothin. Wanna hear another? The big oak table in the kitchen? Musta weighed a haffa ton? Din't it up and take off one fine day. Along come the water and it went clear through the wall. Left a hole clean as a whistle. You c'n see it if you want, where they patcht-it up. Only the table, no one seen it since. Last we know, it was heading for Horse Pasture.

"That time Gramma lost her quilts. She pluckt and cleant them feathers her own self, for her hope chest, when she was just a itty-bitty girl. They din't go no-wheres. They sank. Straight to the bottom. Black as mud and smelt-ta high heaven. River water! That's the dirtiest slimiest stinkenest stuff that there is."

The farm had been divided up when the old couple died; not enough left for anyone to make a living on. Luellen's father farmed, but everyone else in the family went to work in town. Her mother had a job on the breakfast and lunch shift in a diner.

"One day she comes home from work and finds him setting and rocking hisself by the cabinet radio. Like he's went and done all his chores and he ain't got a care in the worlt. Well, she knows darn well he ain't done neither—on count of she seen the cows mooing and looking over their backs; the way they do when they expect-ta get milkt. And she's all set-ta open her mouth and yell at him; only just then he stops rocking and he turns his head, real slow. He looks acrost at her and he drops his eyes and she sees where he's looking at. A piece a paper under the lamp, and it's a note in his hantwriting.

"Sometimes Pa, he din't talk to nobody for weeks on ent, but he never left no notes before.

"So she picks it up and starts-ta read it, and he lays back and shuts his eyes. Thumping 'n rocking, thumping 'n rocking.

" 'I have drank lye,' is what it sait."

Our secret ambition was to send for everything advertised in the back pages of Luellen's magazines:

Give Your Hair a Chance to Win You Love and Romance

"Taboo"—The Forbidden Nightie—*Black* as a moonless night/All the allure of *Gay Paree*

Are You Lucky? (If not, why not?)

The trouble was, we had no money. I wasn't getting paid, though Reuben gave me a quarter now and then for standing in front of the television set. The TV reception in Lungo wasn't so hot; sometimes we couldn't get a picture unless someone stood in a certain spot and held a hand out on top of the set. It had to be just that particular spot, and it had to be a *person.* Usually that *person* was me.

And Luellen's only source of income now was going down to the beach and collecting pop bottles so she could turn them in for the deposit. But she hated the beach; she was allergic to the sun, she said. Her skin really was delicate: spun floss. She had to wear a big straw coolie hat that Reuben hated; he said it made her look like a lamp under a shade.

Dykstra, the crabby old shopkeeper in town, gave her credit on the sly. I think he had a crush on Luellen. Her cigarettes and magazines, lipstick, nail polish, eyebrow pencil, wavy hairpins. (Their coppery glint was not so bright as her hair.) He sold bruised fruit, sour milk, stale bread, calamine lotion, insect spray, mothballs, mouthwash, bandages—such dusty odds and ends as summer people might ask for—and spirals of sticky brown flypaper hung in the window all year round.

Even Dykstra sometimes wanted money on account; then we had to start digging through the garbage— eggshells, orange and banana peels, wet coffee grounds —looking for butts. Luellen lighted them up, one squashed stub pressed to another, inhaling until her eyes all but crossed over her nose.

It made her look as if she was trying to concentrate.

"Esti? Hey, Esti? Here, lookit. Read this." Handing over her magazine.

I leaned on my stomach and elbows and began to read aloud:

" '*Smiling, Boyd brought his face close to mine. . . .*' "

"Boyd," she said. "Boyd. What do you think?" She

was musing over possible names for the baby. "Don't that sound like a real *boy's* name? Boyd?"

" ' . . . *brought his face close to mine. Our two lips met, and clung. It was instantaneous, inevitable, irresistible. Like the force of gravity. Or, I thought, a force greater still. The force . . .* ' "

Luellen grabbed the pages from me and clasped them to her breast, reciting with a solemn solid-blue stare (she knew the rest by heart):

". . . ' *the force a love.* ' "

She waited for me to say something. People were always waiting for me to say something. It made me nervous. I could never tell what it was they wanted me to say.

"Four lips," I said. "Shouldn't it be: *'Our four lips met and clung'?* Two and two makes four."

Luellen hugged the pages flat against her. Her eyes rolled toward their red-gold brows.

"Ugh," she said. "Esti Esti Esti." —I thought it sounded like *tsk tsk tsk* when people repeated my name that way. —"Esti Esti Esti. I should know better'n to ask you. You don't appreciate nothing. You're not susceptible."

Lungo had a reputation.

What happened was, a local resident turned up in the trunk of an automobile left standing on a church parking lot, with two flat tires, for an unusually long time. And the church was clear on the other side of Chicago. The papers carried the story for weeks and kept harping on Lungo, Lungo. I think that was how come my boyfriend Donny showed up as often as he did; he was hoping to get a look at some gangsters. That's what he wanted to be when he grew up.

Donny was very good-looking. So good-looking I was surprised the first time I saw him; I never saw anyone else who surprised me. It was in the high-school corridor at lunchtime, and everyone was fetching up brown paper bags that smelled of tuna fish and bananas and slamming tin lockers, and there was Donny—tall and dark and built like a statue. No kidding. His shoulders and chest were as muscular as armor—a breastplate. His jaw was hinged. He had that kind of curly grape-cluster hair that statues have, and his nose was like a statue's too; smashed. Flattened in a fight. I wouldn't say it spoiled his looks, but it made them moody.

You would have taken him for Greek or Italian, but Donny was Bohemian. I wasn't sure what that meant. His father was a janitor and they lived in a basement flat with painted pipes in the ceiling. Two weeks every summer they took a vacation, farther up the lake, in Michigan. The old man sat on a blanket in his undershirt, a handkerchief knotted around his head, reading his newspapers in thick foreign type. He was a whole foot shorter than Donny; his glasses were so thick they glowed; his legs stretched on the sand were bony and blue-white. But he beat the tar out of Donny. I never saw him do it, but I saw him threaten—looking up at his son, lustrously, sliding his belt out of his pants.

Whenever Donny borrowed his father's car he scratched it up. He drove too fast, and half the time he wasn't even looking where he was going; he was looking behind him, watching for cops.

"Do you think that's a squad car? Do you think he's tailing me?"

He ducked his head into his leather jacket and squinted at the lights in the rearview mirror.

In it I could see the rectangle of his forehead, his frowning eyebrows, an edge of curly hair. I figured he must be looking at himself. Donny was forever looking at himself. In mirrors, in plate-glass windows, in gum machines. When we ate at the chili parlor, at the counter with its bottles of red pepper sauce and bowls of oyster crackers (why they called those pellets oyster crackers I never did know)—when we sat on the stools, under the hard lights, I could catch him squinting at himself, I swear, in the spoons.

For his favorite pose, though, he turned his face aside; jaw angled, eyebrow lifted, frowning at himself over his collar. Its raised tips sharp against his cheeks.

He jammed his hands into the pockets over his stomach, making fists.

"Do you think I look tough enough? Does my nose make me look tough?"

At the pink hotel, a parking lot overlooked the water, and Friday and Saturday nights from sunset on it was full of cars—windows rolled up, no matter how hot it was; heads close together behind steering wheels. Striped raccoon tails dangled from the antennas, as jumpy as if they were alive; car radios jittered like insects in weeds.

To the south, the mills gave off a thick orange glow, mightier than the sinking clouds. Lights squiggled on the surface of the water. Chicago rose from the horizon the way heat rises from the highway: staggering, shimmering. You could never be sure you were seeing it because it was *there*.

Donny dug inside my blouse. I pushed his hand away. He forced it down.

"Your skin is so snooth and creany," he said.

I'm sorry, but that's what he said. He was breathing hard through his mashed-in nose.

He smelled of leather jacket, cigarettes, hair tonic, fresh-pressed khakis, and a T-shirt that had dried outdoors, on the line. But mostly of hair tonic. It got all over my hands.

Sooner or later we had to get out and inspect the damage.

I struck matches and held them up so Donny could see. He crouched, running his fingers over doors, fenders, dents, creases, scratches in ten different colors—paint he had taken along, off other cars.

"Do you think that's a new one? Do you think I just did that?"

His voice was anxious, pleading with me, the way he did in the car; his jaw had a glassy edge. Maybe that was the matches.

"I'm in for it now. I'm gonna catch it for sure. My old man'll pin it on me, all right. He's gonna lick the daylights outta me."

Smooth heavy waves slapped back and forth—water slopped in a tub. In all the parked cars, leather jackets were creaking. By this time, someone was bound to get fed up with us—all this crouching and sneaking and whispering. A window would roll down, a head would pop out.

A sudden jeering burst of song.

"Hey, you creeps. Whatsa matter wichew. Whaddayawant? Go on. Ged oudda here. Beat it. What are you? Morons? Peeping Toms?"

At the funeral, my father was reconciled with his family. They sat under the cemetery canopy, all in a row; the two daughters on one side, the mother in the middle; Uncle Abie, my father, Uncle Reuben shoulder to shoulder, their necks hot above their white prayer shawls. Especially Uncle Abie's, all red baubles of pimples. The black circles of skullcaps looked small on their heads.

Flor's fox fur dangled from her shoulders, staring straight at me. Her husband, the dentist, had been killed overseas not long before—some kind of explosion. I wasn't supposed to ask or say. Her face was in her handkerchief, the creature shuddering on her back. Honey kept eyeing her sister out of the side of her face, over her spit-curled cheek, the way she did when they sat together at the piano and she looked to Flor to let her know when to turn the page. Every once in a while she took her handkerchief out of her sleeve (Honey was never without a handkerchief tucked up her sleeve, the tight part, where it gripped her vaccination mark) and dabbed first at Flor's nose and then at her own. Her black dress was rusty and smelly under the arms.

A clump of men moved forward, feet crunching grass. Their two rows of heads made an aisle. I craned my neck, trying to get a look; all the grownup legs in the way. That was when the commotion started.

A woman was pushing through the small crowd, crying out as she came. It didn't sound like grief; more like someone in a hurry. She was shaking her fist—that was the first time I saw anyone actually shaking a fist—as if she had been running for a bus and saw it pulling away.

Her thick short legs rocked her from side to side.

People were glancing about, turning heads, looking over shoulders.

I pulled my mother's sleeve. Who's that, Mommy? Who's that lady?

My mother pressed her lips together and stared in front of her, the way she did when I had asked what I shouldn't. So I knew I wasn't going to get any answer. Some shameful secret. Not for me to know.

But the woman wasn't anyone; not to us, anyhow. Someone who hung around the funeral chapel—they had had trouble with her before—weeping, posing as a mourner, hitching rides to the cemetery.

With a howl—indignation—outrage—she threw herself onto the ground, face down, beating her fists on the grass.

On the way home I sat in the back seat of the car on Boaz Benjamin's lap. He was smoking a cigar. From time to time he leaned forward to tap the white ash out the window, then sat back and pushed the cigar into the O of his mouth. The hot wind was scattering the scanty hairs on his head. His face was round, like his mouth, and when his eyebrows went up, they became pink fleshy wrinkles—just like a baby's.—*Ish that sho?* That was the way Boaz talked. Rolling the cigar in his mouth and raising his wrinkles.—*You don't shay?* As if he was too polite to mention it, but he really didn't believe you.

His shirt, the necktie spouting from the rift in his vest, his cigar and the cylinders of his fingers, were banded in gold.

In those days, going to the cemetery was like going to the country; a long dreary ride. Stubbled fields, fertilizer. Insects splattered the windshield before you got a chance to see what they were. Red Burma Shave signs shot by. I hung my head out the window, getting sick on the greenish smell of cigars. But that was to be expected; I always got carsick.

I don't know if I should tell this part.

That night, or a few nights after (the family was in mourning at my grandmother's house; now there were sheets on the mirrors too), I was outside in the backyard, catching fireflies. The grass was slippery and limp and juicy with mosquitoes. They were sprinkled like dew. In the alley, a streetlamp was lighting up the branches of a tree, making the leaves green glass.

Fireflies spurted and dimmed, dimmed and spurted, as if someone were trying to light matches, scratching sparks against a wall.

I looked at the stars. You could still see stars in the city then, and my father had told me how far they were. Millions and billions and trillions of miles. There was something thrilling and chilling in the sound. *Zillions.* But all at once, looking up at the sky, I knew what it meant. I felt it. It went right through me. Only for an instant—but that was enough.

Forever.

Everything. Everyone.

It didn't seem right, it didn't seem fair. It was no help either if you were a tree, or a rock. Not even the earth. Not even the sun.

For. Ever.

It felt like car sickness, only not just in my stomach. All my insides; lurching with motion. Spinning spinning like all those dying worlds up there. I threw myself onto the grass, beating my fists. The earth was spongy and wet. I must have looked like the poor crazy lady who invited herself to my grandfather's funeral.

Donny loved to hear Reuben's stories about Boaz Benjamin.

"Boaz was always like one of the family. He courted my sister Flor before she ever met that dentist guy, that poor son-of-a-bee. He wanted to marry Flor himself. But my mother, she should rest in peace, she thought Flor could do better; someone with a profession. Someone with ambition. Not that she had anything against Boaz personally, except he never had a job. Not that anyone knew of. If you really wanna know what his occupation was, I'll tell you. It was hanging around on the porch steps, waiting for Flor, that's what.

"But take it from me, he had plenty ambition, Boaz. He had too much ambition to work, is all. You got to hand it to him. He stuck to his guns. He kept his principles. That's what I call intestinal fortitude. —That's guts, to you.

"These guys he knew were buying and selling meat

on the black market. That was during the war. It was a racket; it wasn't legal. You could make a bundle, and you could get yourself bumped off too, just as easy, if you didn't watch out. Well, one day these pals of his get tipped off that so-and-so is thinking of hijacking a shipment they got coming in at such-and-such a time. And what do you think they do? They send Boaz down there, to guard the Meat.

"Some pals! Boaz! —That's a laugh. You never saw Boaz, but he's kind of a little fat guy, and he must of been bald since the day he was born. Turn a soup bowl upside down, and you got the top of his head. Boaz! — What does he know? But right away he gets a bright idea. You know my brother, Sammy, don't you? Sammy's a husky guy, right? A real bruiser. So Boaz decides Sammy should go along. And Sammy, like a dope, he goes. Because Sammy—what does he know?

"Now here's the Meat, see, sitting in a trailer at the loading dock, waiting to get unloaded into the freezer. And here's Boaz and Sammy, strolling up and down, up and down, with their heads in their shoulders and their hands in their pockets. A coupla tough guys. And believe me—you got a loaded gun in your pocket, you'll keep your hand on it too.

"But Boaz, he's jumpy. He stops at every little noise. Every two seconds he looks at Sammy:

" 'Shh. Sammy. What's that?'

"And Sammy looks at him and shrugs. You know Sammy:

" 'I didn't hear nothing.'

"Well, it could of been two minutes, it could of been two hours. They're shaking the whole time. Their teeth are tap-dancing. It's plenty cold out too, I want you to

know. They don't know what to shiver from first. Some
tough guys.

"Finally Boaz gets another idea: 'You know what,
Sammy? Maybe we should look inside. Make sure everything's all right. We got nothing else to do. Let's you
and me take a look at the Meat.'

"Now Boaz, like I told you, he never had no job. He
never done no dirty work. The only meat he ever seen
was at the butcher's. He don't know what they got in
there—all them cows sawed up and split up and hanging upside down. They got their hoofs and tails on and
all. He takes one look.

" 'My God,' he says. 'There's dead animals in there.'
And he turns kinda pale. Usually Boaz, he's kinda pink.

"And just then he sees something move.

"He looks at Sammy. 'What's that?'

"Sammy shrugs. 'I didn't see nothing.'

"Boaz says, 'Hold still,' and he takes his gun outta his
pocket. He's shaking so bad he's hanging on to it with
both hands.

"He yells, 'Who's there?'

"Naturally nobody says nothing. Naturally.

"So he points his gun into the meat locker, and his
voice and the gun are both shaking. 'Come out. Come
out. I got you covered,' he says. 'Come out with your
hands up or I swear I'll shoot.'

"And just when he gets to *shoot*—all hell breaks loose.
His gun goes off. He don't mean it, only he can't help
it, he's shaking so bad. All he can do is hang on with
both hands and the gun keeps shooting. And here's all
the Meat swinging on the meat hooks. Sammy, he don't
see nothing, but he's shooting too.

"Then all of a sudden, it gets real quiet. You know how

quiet it gets after there's shooting? Well, take it from me, that's what you call *quiet.* They got no more bullets. The Meat is still swinging and they're still shaking. So Boaz looks at Sammy. And Sammy looks at Boaz. And they both turn and take off like a bat outta hell.

"Naturally, there ain't nobody there. There never was. The whole time, they're shooting at nothing. Only hold on—wait a minute. A little while later, and who should come along, but—you guessed it—the hijackers. And whaddayaknow? Here's the Meat sitting there, all by its lonesome, the trailer all set and ready to roll. So they lock her up and load her onto their truck and away they go with the Meat. A whole carload—and it ain't worth nothing, not a red cent.

"Why not? Because it's all shot up, that's *why not.* Who's gonna eat a steak that got bullets in it?

"Word gets around, and these guys are a laughing-stock. Everyone thinks Boaz done it on purpose, to outsmart the thieves. And the next shipment that these pals of his get—it doubles in value right away. Because people, they still want the Meat. These hotels and res-taurants, they gotta stay in business. The gang gets their money out of it all the same. And Boaz, he gets a reputation for being a shrewd operator.

"Not that I'm trying to take nothing away from my brother-in-law Boaz; he's got plenty upstairs. He'll beat this rap too, you'll see. Only Ma, my poor mother, may her soul rest in peace—she'd turn over in her grave if she knew she had a daughter had a husband in trouble with the law.

"And that, believe it or not, is how Boaz Benjamin busted into the rackets and become a big shot. So help me God."

.   .   .

The neighbors kept their blinds down day and night, though the voices of daytime serials—organ swoops and swells—came through the screen. No one seemed to come and go. Sometimes a blonde, in a bathrobe and hair curlers, with a sleepy puffy face and sketchy eyebrows, came out as far as the porch stoop to throw out the garbage. Donny felt sure there was something fishy. "She's a gun moll. They're hiding out in there." At the beach, he was on the lookout for suspicious characters; sitting on blankets, opening pop bottles, pulling the waxed paper off of sandwiches. Any heavyset swarthy greasy types—barrel chests, meaty shoulders, dark-haired navels—Donny followed with greedy eyes.

"See that guy? No, not that one. That one over there. No, don't look now. Oh God, she turns around and stares. What'd you do that for? You don't wanna tip him off. You got him looking at us now. You tryna get us killed?"

The funny thing is, that was what my Uncle Reuben looked like; only more so. Reuben was swarthier, meatier, hairier than anyone; black with hair; and his cheeks were so blue they looked tattooed. When he rubbed his jaw against Luellen's cheek you could hear beard scraping. He sweated so much he started stripping off his clothes as soon as he walked through the door, wiping his neck and chest with his shirt.

Lest anybody get any ideas, Reuben was a law-abiding citizen; a truck driver, a piano mover. He worked for a local firm and did no long-distance hauling now that he had his "draft deferments," as he called the twins. Reuben had been in the service twice—first at the end

of World War II, and then he almost got shipped to
Korea—and he wanted no more of the Army. But that
was how he had met Luellen, stationed somewhere
down South; Camp Chaffee, if that's the one in Ar-
kansas.

In their wedding picture, crowded onto the wall, his
cheeks had been touched up and smoothed out, and it
didn't look like Reuben. His eyes were brash and glistening. But that was how he looked when he shaved—
sometimes it took him an hour—prowling all over the
house in his shorts and shaving cream, the floors
bouncing under his bare feet.

Luellen didn't like it when he went around "nakitt."

"Oh yeah? I'm the Boss. I can do what I want. Am I
the head of this household or aren't I?"

He snapped the end of his wet towel at her.

—Exactly what he used to do to me, whenever we
went to the beach on family picnics. He would twist his
towel up in both hands—winding it up—and let fly with
one end. It stung like sand. I dearly longed to learn how
(and I wished I could stick two fingers in the corners of
my mouth—the way he could—and tweet); but I never
did get the hang of it, and Reuben, skipping backwards,
out of reach, would laugh at me:

"What're you doing? Flag waving? Whyncha hit me?
Hit me all you want. Hit me hard as you can. Whatsa
matter? Go on. Hit me."

His brown titties bounced on his chest, like sleepy
eyes in his tangle of hair. His wet trunks dripped and
drooped so you could see the white line where his but-
tocks began, and whorls of wet hair clung to his legs.

I never could figure out what grownups saw in
picnics.

That was the way Reuben walked; like a man coming out of the water, heavy and wading up to his thighs. His arms and legs were lavish with hair, lathered and black with hair; he even had hair on his back. It was fur on his chest.

"Aw, Lou? Let's kiss and make up," Reuben would say, still teasing Luellen, sticking out his face at her—his lips cushiony pink in the midst of his shaving cream. Here and there the razor had cut a swath, a blue streak, through the foam on his cheek.

She turned her face aside. "Don't you *Aw, Lou* me, you big ape you."

"Aw, Lou. Are you mad at me?"

Luellen pushed out her lip and stared down her nose. Her blue eyes fused. "That's f'r me-ta know and you-ta find out."

"Luellen? Hey? Luellen? You-hoo?" Reuben waved a hand in front of her face. "Anybody home? Lou-hoo?"

Luellen kept staring; stock-still; white, big-bottomed, a hand on either knee, her head wrapped in braids. In summer, Luellen kept her hair pinned up; she could braid it up, in a trice, with one hand—opening pins in her teeth. Her skin and hair gleamed like embroidery silk on a pillow. Sprigs of red-gold dangled on her neck.

Reuben walked all around her, gawking (I thought), as if he had never seen her before, or anything like her; this mystery, this immovable object.

The fluorescent glow of Blazing Kiss lighted her face.

"Luellen? Luellen? Let your hair down."

It always came to that. That was Reuben's way of making up. And once he got started on it, there was no letting go. He could stand there all day, if he had to; in his shorts and hairy belly, hairy legs; wheedling and whining, feasting his eyes on her. Counting his gold.

"Aw, Lou? Don't be mad? On't-day e-bay ad-may? Oo-lay?" Reuben liked to talk Pig Latin.

And at last, at last, taking pity on him, the corners of her mouth turning up and down at the same time—you could never tell if she was smirking or pouting, hiding her teeth—Luellen would reach up and start pulling pins out of her hair. She tugged at her braids, loosened them a little, and then—a toss of her head, a kind of exultation—all her hair would come tumbling down; slipping down her back, sliding over her shoulders. She kept shaking her head, her hair swaying from side to side, scattering the gleam of red-gold and the smell of shampoo. The way you might grab a branch and shake the leaves, the fragrance, out of a tree.

I was supposed to be helping Tante Malkeh in the kitchen, but the old woman was so jealous of her greasy pots and pans she couldn't stand having anyone else around. If I put a dish away in one place, she'd take it out—slam the cupboard—and put it somewhere else. Another slam. Her Abarbanel hair was still coarse wiry black; her chin tipped up and her nose tipped down, and she seemed to be hiding something behind her pinched shrivelled lips; hoarding like a miser.

Once she came up to me, a big black frying pan in her hand, poking a big black fingernail at my mouth. Her fingers were sharp and misshapen. Then she opened up her own mouth and pointed inside.

"What is it, Tante Malkeh? Are you all right?"

She kept looking up, mouth open, poking her finger first at her mouth and then at mine.

"Are you choking? Are you thirsty? Can I get you a glass of water?"

She put down her frying pan and with two hands— two pointy fingertips—pulled my mouth open and peered inside. Her old eyes lighted up in their sunken depths.

"Kinnehora," she said, clicking her tongue—this to ward off the Evil Eye—and putting her head first to one side, then the other. "So many. So many."

She laid a hand to her cheek. She was admiring my teeth. And she counted them, each and every one, from end to end and top to bottom.

Tante Malkeh had a bird, a parakeet she had found hopping around on the lid of the garbage can, one foot beneath its breast. It was pistachio color with black and white marks on its wings and it perched on her finger —its claws gripping her claw—pecking food from her lips. She mashed it up with her gums and spat it out a little at a time, the bird's beak as quick and secretive as hers. It got so she wouldn't eat with—would hardly talk to—anyone but this Boo-jee; the bird slept in the same room with her, a towel over its cage. Otherwise it would have fussed and fretted all night.

Tante Malkeh snored; sometimes gently, fluttering; sometimes like a man—Reuben, or my father—a terrific roaring rising rip. Every once in a while she would stop snoring altogether, right in the middle of a breath. As if someone had crept into the room and got her by the throat. Donny and I, necking on the couch, on the sticky plastic covers, would break apart; stricken; it was so sudden.

"Onethousanandone. Onethousanandtwo."

Donny would start to count, under his breath, through his nose.

No sound. No breathing. The old woman was hovering there, her dark crop open. What if she was dead? What if she was stealing in, secretly, to discover us?

I started buttoning my blouse.

"Onethousanandfive. Onethousanandsix. Onethousanandseven."

A gasp. A rattle. A rasp. Tante Malkeh was in business again. We let out our breath. Boo-jee scratched the newspapers and gravel at the bottom of its cage. The twins smacked their bottles, the nipples sighed.

Donny was trying to get me down on the couch, trying to get on top of me, sliding his hand up under my skirt. He pushed the bulge in his pants against me; I pushed him away. He sat up, moody, smelling of hair oil. Then he frowned; he turned his face; his jaw hardened. He had caught a glimpse of his flattened profile in a picture frame.

I had to get up at night to go to the bathroom; I had put it off—dreaming about it—as long as I could. I went downstairs and snapped on the hall light, and a man was in the front room. Just sitting there; I couldn't see his face for his hat and his nose. Buttons, a necktie, a belt buckle over his stomach; dark sleeves on the arms of the chair.

A sleeve raised up, a hand reached out, a finger hooked at me.

My bare feet stuck to the spot.

It was the Stranger. The one my mother was forever warning me about. The Stranger who would offer me pennies, candies. The Stranger who would beckon me into his car. The Stranger who would be waiting for me in some dark hallway. I knew all along he would be like this. No face, no words.

A hat, a sleeve, a crooked finger.

The door swung from the kitchen; my mother, pushing her way through, carrying a glass of hot tea. I threw myself at her—my arms reaching for her waist, my face for her apron—and the glass splashed in the dish and both crashed in splinters.

It must have burned her when it spilled, because she shoved me from her and put her finger to her mouth.

Now look what you made me do. What's the matter with you? Get back—get away from me. And watch out for your feet. There's broken glass.

Punitive and protective, that's my mother.

This was really unfair. And I had to *go* too—so bad, it hurt. I looked at her, knowing it was no use trying to explain, and tears began to prickle and sting and run down my cheeks. But almost at the same instant—released, you might say, by the same force—something was prickling and stinging and running down inside my leg. I couldn't help it; couldn't hold it anymore. Couldn't stop one or the other. I was running over. But that wasn't the worst of it. The worst was, you could hear it. Splashing. On the linoleum.

Did you ever notice? They both come out so *hot?*

My mother was staring at me, still sucking on her finger.

Well, that's just about enough out of you, she said. What kind of behavior do you call this? Shame on you. A big girl like you. I intend to speak to your father. I'd be ashamed to show you to anyone—acting up like this.

She leaned down and went on in a whisper. Who do you think that is? That man? That's your Uncle Daniel. That's your daddy's long-lost brother. He was Over There. In the War. He's seen terrible terrible things.

A lot I cared what things he'd seen. All I knew was, he'd seen *me* pee in my pants.

Boaz Benjamin got a kick out of gadgets, and whenever we went to his house, we had to stand in front of lights, with bedsheets behind us, holding still for him while he fiddled with the wobbly legs of his tripod. His wire recorder he liked to run on the sly, while everyone else was talking. Then he would play it for us—sitting back, silently plopping smoke rings—as a surprise. (That shut everybody up.) At the party he gave for Daniel, we all had turns talking into the microphone, saying something for the occasion; then Boaz pulled down the shades and put out the lights and showed home movies he had taken of the family.

The den was like their living room, but darker—it was in the basement—with a dark mirrored wall spackled in glitter; and everything—the bar, the padded stools, the couch, the armchairs, even the lampshades—had been covered in the same zebra-striped fur. I sat squeezed into a corner of the couch; Daniel happened to be in a chair right next to it, holding on to the arm. I had heard something about a number. I didn't see any number. Only a hand, at the end of a sleeve.

Daniel was the only one in a suit and tie, and his black sleeves smelled under the arms, like Honey's black dress, only much stronger. It wasn't a smell I associated with men; my father, with his machine oil when he came from work, his hair oil when he came from the barber; Boaz, with his cigars and sulphury matches. You didn't have to sniff; it was there, it was him. That was one impression. The other was the same I had had the first time I saw a newborn baby—someone held it up to show me. So that was the way they came! In a bag! A baby came in a bag of its own shrunken skin! That was Daniel. Skin. It covered his head, crumpled his brow, lidded his eyes; it ran down the back of his neck and into his collar, and came out at his sleeves and wrinkled his fingers. The parts of him that showed, and the parts that didn't—all the same slack stuff. A paper bag of skin, and almost that color.

Everyone was talking louder than ever because Daniel didn't speak English, and trying out Yiddish on him. He ducked his head into his watermelon (Boaz loved watermelon, had to have it on the table; huge slices of watermelon, red and green and white boats), looking from one to the next and spitting out the slippery seeds behind his thumb. When he opened his mouth and shut his eyes his lips seemed to shrink and his eyes disappeared into skin. It looked as if it hurt.

I knew how he felt. What was he supposed to make of all these Abarbanels, mired in black hair; their blue beards, their honeycombed cheeks; their loud lively angry-laughing voices, all going at once. Maybe to him the voices sounded scrambled together, quacking and gobbling, the way they sounded whirling backwards on Boaz's coppery wire spool. How was he supposed to know what the shouting was about. I wondered if he could tell any better than I could, what it meant: if they were mad at each other and about to start throwing dishes and coming to blows—or just having a good time.

Up on the screen, people walked into the camera and waved, walked away from the camera and waved. Honey, playing with her old dog (it was buried in the backyard by now), clicking her cheek at it, with coy spit-curled glances—holding up a ball out of its reach. Flor, showing off her fur coat, smiling and shading her eyes with her hand. Her eyes were large and symmetrical and beaded with lashes, and her fingers dripped polished nails and rings; but you couldn't tell which was her neck and which was her chin.

A man slouched in shirt sleeves and suspenders, wiping his lips.

Who's that? I wanted to know, pointing to the screen. People were getting up and going for food, and their heads got in the way of the fizzing white beam. The film was flapping in the projector like a piece of paper caught in a fan. Boaz frowned over it, his ears in the light pink and plushy. And it was a good thing no one heard me, or let on, because I remembered. —It was Honey's boyfriend, the one who used to sit on the couch with her—between the two goggle-eyed dolls, propped on their pillows—holding hands. He hadn't showed up in some time.

Ig-bay Outh-may, was what Reuben called me.

The lights hadn't been out for very long before Daniel started falling asleep.

First his sleeve slid off the arm of the couch. I poked it with my elbow and it pulled right back. I hadn't meant to wake him, but, in no time, it happened again. His arm began slipping sideways. I looked at him out of the corner of my eye, and, sure enough, his head was slipping. I held still. Pretty soon his fingers loosened their grip, his hand hung over my lap—over my leg, the bare part between my skirt and my knee. So I pulled my skirt down and that woke him again.

He sat up and held onto the chair. I sat up too, and folded my hands in my lap and looked at the screen as hard as I could. But I wasn't watching, I was waiting. Every time the hand dropped and the fingers dangled, I pulled down my skirt and squeezed out of the way. I tried to make my movements as accidental as his. Maybe I would squirm toward the other side as soon as the hand got going; maybe I would wait until it hung over my lap, and nudge his elbow with my elbow, inch by inch. As if I couldn't help fidgeting in my seat—any more than he could help dropping off in his.

But once, when I put my head down and tipped my face to sneak a look at him, I saw that he was doing the same. Out of the side of his head, over his wrinkled cheek, one whole white eyeball bared at me.

Skinned.

It disappeared. Back in the bag. His head shut into his shoulders, his chin sank into his neck. Now there was only a bald head and the screen.

Oh oh. Look who's falling asleep already.

I'll be darned. Look at that. Just like Pa.

Late at night, Reuben got a call from Honey. A hospital in Uptown had telephoned her. Honey lived with Flor, and had ever since their mother died; but not even the family knew the number of Boaz's private line, and the other phone was listed in Honey's name. —My grandfather's name. I told you it was very unusual; the only one like it in the city directory. My father and his brothers had lopped off the tail, but Honey had kept her maiden name intact; maybe she was expecting to change it. The doctor on duty looked her up in the book. A patient with that same name had died there that night. The doctor was wondering if she might be, or would know of, any relation? Because all they knew was the name. And the deceased had had a number on his arm.

Reuben marched straight through the house, straight in the front door and straight out the back, looking neither left nor right; dragging his tie out of his shirt, off his neck. He was wearing his dark suit and a black paper skullcap—the kind they hand out at synagogues and funeral services—and sweat was leaking down the sides of his face. His blue cheeks were gritty as gunmetal. His feet still sounded as if they were trampling boards.

"Ouch!"

The screen door slammed behind him.

There were no springs on the door, and every time it shut someone winced and went Ouch.

A lot of things had turned out to be wrong with the house, minor annoyances—faucets, light fixtures, flaky plaster—and Reuben was in no position to complain. Boaz had done him a favor getting the house in the first place. And in the second place Boaz was in jail.

"You tell. That fat. Lazy. Red-headed. Good-for-nothing. Hillbilly. Tell her she should get herself dressed and get out here. If she knows what's good for her. On the double. You hear me? And I don't mean maybe. I got company coming. It don't look right."

He was talking to me, but stretching his neck over the edge of his collar, pitching his voice hoarsely toward the bedroom window. Through the screen it was easy enough to see the fan on the chair, turning and droning, and, on the bed, Luellen's two big white calves—curved and luminous as half-moons.

Her toes were spread, drying her nail polish.

"You got that? All right then. Let's see some action. I want results around here." Handing me his jacket and walking off, rubbing his hands together, his rubber heels flashing. His back was so wet with sweat the colors of flesh and black hair showed through his shirt.

Luellen had stayed home because she had morning sickness; I had stayed to look after the twins. Hardly anyone had gone to Daniel's funeral. My grandfather had no other relatives here; Daniel himself had been all that was left of his family from the old country. And even the Abarbanels were not what they used to be. All those old cousins and aunts, like Tante Malkeh, who never missed a funeral—any funeral, it didn't matter whose (sitting with their black heads together, in their black dresses; an endless supply, it had seemed to me, since I could never tell them apart)—all of them, it turned out, had all along been dying off themselves. And it was a long drive in the heat from the gates of Waldheim to Lungo.

"Oh yeah. And another thing. Esti?"

Reuben stopped and looked back. I waited.

"Esti? You could smile sometime. How about it? It don't cost nothing. It don't hurt. It ain't against the law."

"Okay, Uncle Reuben."

"*Okay,* she says." He threw up his hands. "Don't just stand there and say okay. Ile-smay!"

It was hot hot hot. Even the grass hurt your eyes. The neighbors' sprinkler shuddered over the lawn, flinging up glittering fans of water. Tante Malkeh was carrying food out from the kitchen, banging the screen door. Flies stuck to the hunched black back of her dress— bitter-green, greedy-bright, flashing like nailheads. Card tables were lined up to make one long table on the grass. There were pop bottles, seltzer bottles, beer bottles; bottles of wine with purple grapes on the labels; bottles of amber. —What Reuben called the "strong stuff." He kept it for company—he was strictly a beer drinker himself—and Donny had got into the habit of sampling it. Little by little. I had been filling up the bottle with tea.

"How would it be if I dropped it and busted it?" Donny said. "It'll look like an accident. He won't get the goods on us then."

Cars were arriving, scraping gravel.

Uncle Abie and his wife were already seated at the table, waiting for the food. Abie kept frowning backwards over his shoulder, his frown and his hump so meaty he looked insulted. Flor sat at the end, where Honey had put her, in a black dress and black glasses. She wore them to hide her eyes, swollen and tender from weeping. A gold watch, a man's watch, dangled from one heavy arm, and three big rings—nuts and bolts of gold—hung from a chain around her neck. Boaz's jewelry: she had taken a vow to wear it next to her, night and day, until they let him out.

Honey winked at me and drew me aside; she wanted to get at her money. Honey never kept money in her purse, only on her person. Whenever I used to go shopping with her and it came time to pay, we had scenes like this: me standing in front of her—giving such cover as I could—and warning her in case I saw someone coming; and Honey digging and feeling in private places. Reaching deep down into her bra, or hiking up her skirts and tugging at the rolled garters that held up her stockings. Her dough was stashed away in all that scented talc and pillowy flesh.

"Oh boy, it's hot. Phew! It was murder out there. All those tombstones, they're so darn bright. And poor Flor, she cried her eyes out. Anything sad makes her think of You-Know-Who." The lawyers had cautioned the sisters not to talk about Boaz's case, and Flor got upset if anyone so much as said his name.

Honey's hair was red these days, medicinal red, the color of the cough syrup on the shelves at Dykstra's; her face was as powdered and pitted as the vaccination mark on her arm. She clicked a spit-curled cheek at me—a sidelong glance from her sparkling eyes.

I heard something snap, and Honey held up a folded green wad. She blew the powder off and pressed it into my hand. "Mum's the word, kiddo. Button your lip. Give this to your Uncle Reuben. He'll know what for."

Reuben was going around the table filling shot glasses for his guests. Donny and I looked at each other —he was pouring from the old opened bottle. We held up our glasses and tucked in our heads, ready to nod and mumble over a prayer.

The screen door slammed like a hammer.

It wasn't Tante Malkeh this time; it was Luellen. Emerging from the house at last in her wide coolie hat and tight shiny dress. Especially tight about the hips. Her wedding dress; I recognized it from the picture. And the pose I recognized too; Luellen's eyes cast down under her hat, her two hands clutching a bouquet of cigarettes and matches. It was an iridescent material, the kind that looks pink sometimes and sometimes purple, depending on how it catches the light; and as she moved toward the table, changing colors, you could hear her thighs rubbing together inside her dress.

"Oh, Her Highness," Reuben said, and held out his glass. "What're you wearing that hat for?" he asked right away—glaring at her in the glare of the sun. His skullcap was pushed back on his springy hair. "Didn't I tell you not to wear that hat?"

I hadn't thought of it till then, but most of the family had never been to Reuben's house before; had hardly been exposed to his hospitality—or to Luellen. The twins sat side by side in twin strollers, peering out from under canopies and mosquito netting.

"Isn't that the *sweetest* dress!" Cousin Shirley said, as Luellen sat herself down with a sort of crackle. "But you must be so *hot,* dear. And with *stock*ings on."

Luellen's smile hid her teeth; her lips glimmered.

The holes in the straw hat spattered light over her face. "I hafta put a girdle on, anyways, if I wanna squeeze into this dress. So I might as well go whole hog," she said.

"Hey, Luellen? That's how you say it—Luellen? Here, you want a snifter?" Cousin Harry poured for her. "We are about to partake." Shirley was the Abarbanel of the pair—heavy and dark, with Cleopatra-style black wings around her eyes. Harry was bespectacled, grinning and thin.

Again we ducked our heads. Donny pinched my leg; the men stumbled through a quick prayer. Donny drank in one gulp and started choking before he could set down his glass.

Reuben reached over and slapped him on the back. "Better watch it. Take it easy. That's the *strong stuff.*"

Luellen was taking small sips, her brows skimming over the rim. She had drawn them dark with pencil, and it made her look as if she was considering.

"Call this *strong?*" she said. "Huh. It ain't so *strong.* I wisht you could taste the stuff my gran-daddy uset-ta make. If you think this here is *strong.*"

"Oh. Your gran-daddy—I mean your grandfather—made al-co-hol? Really? That's fascinating." Cousin Shirley looked all around the table, moving her face as well as her eyes. "Harry? Did you hear that? Isn't that fascinating?"

"And I don't mean-ta brag or nothin," Luellen said. "But if you swallowt some a that you'd know what was *strong.* That darn near ript the lining right outta your throat."

"What do you call it?" Harry asked. "Is that what you call fire water?"

"Har-ree. That's In-dians. Nobody's talking about In-dians."

"Well, what do you call it then? Red-eye? White light-ning?"

Under the wide hat, Luellen's face was turning like the fan, slowly but surely from side to side.

"I know! *Moonshine.* Isn't that so?" Cousin Shirley turned on Luellen with aggressive Abarbanel eyes. "That's what they call it. Moonshine, Harry."

Luellen kept shaking her head, her smile sinking into her cheeks and pushing out her lip. "We never callt it nothin. Not that I know of. Just the Jug. That's what Gran-daddy sait. Go git the Jug."

"Ask a foolish question," Reuben said.

Honey's boyfriend started to laugh. He laughed very hard, doubling up, holding on to his chest. He laughed so hard, he seemed to be choking—even crying. There were tears in his eyes. His head bent lower, lower; his shoulders got higher and higher. He was hacking—racking—hawking—wheezing; and then finally he was retching. He sounded disgusted, sick and tired of him-self.

Everyone sat and stared at the streaks of hair on top of his head.

He was the same boyfriend of old; he had been in the Southwest and in a TB sanitarium. He sat back and took off his glasses—his face all of a sudden long and tallowy —and Honey wiped his "poor forehead" with the hanky from her sleeve.

It got quiet; something that never used to happen at family gatherings. Abie pointed for someone to please pass the bread, and his hand chopped at his big chewing cheek, swatting a fly. The sprinkler was shooting darts, clashing swords. Ch. Ch. Ch. A garden hose hissed in the grass. The twins sucked and squeezed at their pacifiers, reminding me of Luellen lighting up butts. Their two pairs of eyes blue and bulging, like hers, and their lids—like hers—delicate and violet and radiant with veins.

Flor leaned on the table in her dark glasses and gold chains. The part in her black hair seemed wider and whiter than ever, and her upper arms were as wobbly as thighs.

"Well, I bet that stuff your grandfather made could sure give you one swell heck of a hangover," Harry said. "I bet you wouldn't soon forget it."

"What'll give you a hangover"— Shirley glanced at him and then at his glass—"what'll give you a hangover is sitting in this hot sun and drinking"—she lifted the bottle and looked at the label—"seltzer water and Mogen David wine."

"*Raw egg,*" Luellen said. "That's what you want. That's the sekritt. I woon't fret no more about them hangovers if I was you. I've yet to see it fail. It'll come right up if you give him raw egg."

Reuben had not taken his eyes off Luellen. His face was as glistening as their gaze, and his damp hair stuck to his forehead.

"What're you wearing that hat for? I asked you."

"I tolt you. I ain't suppost-ta be expost-ta the sun. I'm susceptible."

"I'm sure you are." This from Shirley. "You're so fair, dear."

"I got allergies," Luellen said.

"Allergies! That's a hot one. Listen to this, will you?" Reuben said. "Who ever heard of a hillbilly that got allergies? There ain't no such thing. Where she comes from, all they know is tapeworm and hookworm because they ain't got no shoes on, and that tricky-whoo-see-whatsis that they get from their pigs. Allergies! Get a load of her. She's putting on airs. She never even heard of allergies until she married me."

Luellen's cleavage was quivering. Her flesh in the aqua dress gave off a shimmer of white, tinted the color of skin in a swimming pool.

"Just because we don't know no better!" she said.

Harry laughed. Luellen looked surprised, then a little nervous; then the corners of a smile tucked into her cheeks. It wasn't often she found out she had made a joke.

"Is it true?" Cousin Shirley leaned over the table and lowered her voice. "Is it true, what they said today in the eulogy? About Daniel? First the pogrom, and all of them getting killed off that way? And then the aunt that was taking care of him dying in an epidemic? And then that Russian farmer that got hold of him? And then the Russian Army. Which side were the ones that made him a prisoner? Weren't they fighting each other? I can't keep it straight. And then the Germans. And the camps. My God. How could anyone survive that and be a normal person and lead a normal life?"

"What kind of normal person?" Reuben said. "What kind of normal life?"

Honey's glance dropped to her cheek. "Speak no ill of the dead."

"Who's speaking ill? I ain't speaking no ill. I'm just saying. That whole cockeyed business—that *was* his life. He didn't have no other. Maybe it's just as well it's all over and done with. What's the use a talking? Let him rest. We don't know nothing about it. We ain't ever gonna know."

"Thank God." Shirley shivered.

"Gee Eff," Honey said. Everyone looked at the table. "The old country—they can keep it."

"God bless America is all I can say." Harry held up his glass.

"You can say that again."

"Amen."

"That goes double."

Donny drank too. It was getting so I could smell wine on his breath. His skullcap was pushed back, same as Reuben's, and his face had that bright finish of sweat.

Every once in a while the screen door slammed and Tante Malkeh came out, the little peeping green bird perched on her shoulder. She slammed the door the way she banged the pots and pans—as if she meant to; it was her opinion. Each time she turned to go back in, there were all the flies stuck to her dress.

One of the twins had started to cry, and Luellen pulled it onto her lap. The baby was climbing up the front of her in its pins and diaper, rosy toes prodding her stomach, fingers twisting her earlobes and the knob of her nose, yanking and tangling in her red hair.

"It's going to break your pearls if you don't watch out."

"Those are *cultured* pearls," Reuben said. He sounded mad about something, staring at Luellen with fixed intentions, his eyes fringed and glistening. All of a sudden he said:

"Let your hair down, Luellen. Show 'em what it looks like. Show 'em your hair."

"Shh. Cut it out. You'll embarrass Luellen."

Reuben gave Honey his who's-asking-you look.
"Don't worry. Luellen don't embarrass that easy.
C'mon," he said, and hiccuped into his hand. "It ain't
that great of a favor. Let your hair down. What're you
hiding it for? With that dumb stupid hat?"

That did it. Picking on her hat. Luellen's lip trembled
luminously. She gazed down at her breasts, her eyes two
big blue blurs, light dabbling on her cheeks.

The soapy-yellow smell of citronella came from a
smoking candle on the table. The sprinklers were making prisms, rainbows—pink, purple, turquoise—the
colors of her dress.

"More?" Cousin Harry grabbed a bottle by the neck.
"Who wants more?"

Reuben was blowing his nose, honking into his hanky
out of one dark nostril at a time. (They were like his
mother's, scrolls on a violin.) He leaned forward to stow
the handkerchief in his hip pocket, and, as he did, came
a brusque noise. If the table hadn't been quiet right
then, no one would have heard.

Everyone pretended not to, anyhow. "More? Anybody? More seltzer? More pop? Wine? Beer? What'll it
be, folks? Speak up."

Harry rose to pour. And just as we were sitting like
that, all looking toward Harry and holding out our
glasses (he might have been snapping a picture or
proposing a toast), Uncle Reuben leaned forward,
shifted—magisterially—onto one buttock; and did it
again.

Longer. Louder. More declamatory.

Cousin Harry went on pouring. Wine slurped and
gurgled in the green stomach of the bottle. But there

was no doubt about it this time; this was on purpose, even if it had been an accident before. —Reuben sat back with a grunt of satisfaction, almost achievement. Like someone who has made his point, delivered a rebuttal, shown who was Boss; had the last word.

"Goddammit-to-hell!"

Uncle Abie spoke up for the first time, his head sunk like a musket ball between his shoulders. His hand swatted his brow.

"Ain't nobody else getting bit up around here? Ain't these blankety-blank flies going after nobody but me?"

It was too hot for necking on the couch—the plastic slipcovers felt sticky—so Donny and I were on the floor. The fan blew over our faces. The air was black cotton. Insects were simmering in the grass and bumping into the screens—buzzing and sizzling as if they were getting electrocuted, or plopped in frying pans. Reuben and Luellen had gone out for the evening when their guests left; Tante Malkeh was snoring, the twins sucking on their bottles. Boo-jee was still getting settled down in its cage.

Donny got up to take off his undershirt. That's what he said. But when he stood, that was all he had on; nothing but his undershirt. He was naked from the waist on down.

This was the first time I'd seen it. Oh sure, I'd seen it poking in his pants plenty of times; felt it pushing up against me; even, once or twice, grasped it in my hand. But I mean *seen* it. Really to get a look at.

It was big—big—bigger than I could have guessed; thick, dark, swollen; and sticking up—curved, stiffened —like a dog's tail between its legs.

I felt awfully sorry for Donny. I'd had no idea it was anything like that. No wonder! No wonder he acted so funny. So anxious, so anguished. —He stood there, his face hanging, heated; angry, ashamed, almost abject. Maybe that was how he looked when his father took a strap to him.

I wanted to say something, to console him; but couldn't think of anything to say. Maybe it was better to say nothing at all. Just pretend I didn't notice.

He stripped the T-shirt from his shoulders and rolled it up and threw it aside, a damp rag, and then with a sobbing sound flopped down on top of me; his face on my chest.

I wrapped my arms around his head—which was what I thought he wanted—though the point of his chin was sticking in my breastbone.

"No, no, your *legs,*" he said. "Put your *legs* around me."

His head struggled out of the grip I had on it; his medal dangled from his neck. "Put it in," he whispered.

He rocked on me. "In. In. In."

"What? Where? Where do you want me to put it?"

He groaned and all but banged his head on me. *"Where?* she asks. Do I have to tell you *where?"*

"You mean *that?"* I said. *"There? That'll* never fit *there."*

"Then *make* it fit."

He was grinding and butting, and sweat was sprinkling out of the clumps of his hair. *"Make* it fit," he begged me. A great drop of sweat rolled down his ear, along his jaw, and splashed on me.

"Oh, no," he said. "Oh, NO. OH, NO."

His head lay against my neck. I stared at his curly hair. I was afraid to ask what had happened.

"Donny? Donny? Are you all right?"

"Shh!" He lifted his head. Light striped his face. A squeal of tires, screeching brakes, and a car stopped right outside. Headlights flooded the screen door.

"Cops!" Donny said. "It's the cops. It's a raid." He rolled off me. "Keep quiet. Get down."

"How can I get down? I'm on the floor."

He grabbed his pants and started crawling. I followed, picking up clothes as I went. A car door was slamming again and again and voices were raised as if in broad daylight.

"All right for you," Luellen said.

The screen door popped; she came hobbling in. I thought she might be drunk, from the way she kept leaning to one side. Then she stopped and took off her shoe—the heel was broken—and went hopping along on one bare foot, the other lifted behind her, the shoe in her hand.

The door popped again. —Reuben, unbuttoning his shirt and taking off his tie. Luellen didn't turn around when she heard him, but a righteous little shudder went through her, all the way up to her chin.

"C'mon, c'mon. Don't be that way. Is that the way you're gonna be?"

Her dress was crackling and shining across the

beam, and Reuben snapped the tail of his necktie at it.

"Take that back." Luellen turned around, the shoe raised to her shoulder.

"It was only an accident. Honest." He put up his hands.

"I know you," Luellen said. "You done it on purpose. Don't gimme that. Think I don't know you?"

"I did not."

"You did so."

"All right, so I did. Wanna make something of it?" He went on unbuttoning, and snapped the tie at her again.

The shoe flew. Reuben ducked. It bounced off the door with a thud.

"Jeez," Donny whispered.

We were behind the couch, on our knees. The car headlamps lighted up the doorway.

"Oh? So you wanna fight, huh? Good. Let's fight." Tearing open his shirt, exposing the big black bay of his chest. He put up both hands in front of his face, and in the light his eyes were leering between his fists and his hair.

Luellen took off her other shoe, hitched up her shoulder, stuck out her chin—and threw. Another thud. This time the pictures rattled. Reuben grabbed for her, slapping, open-handing, his chin out too; and his fingers must have caught in her pearl choker. Because the next thing you know, things were rolling around on the rug and rattling under the couch.

"Jeez," Donny whispered.

"Now look what you done." Luellen's eyes were like the little bright beads all over the floor.

"Aw, Lou. Aw, Lou." Reuben took a step toward her, holding out burly arms. I don't know whether he meant to or not, but he stumbled and sank to his knees right in front of her.

"Don't be mad?" he said. "Please pretty please?" Kneeling, looking up, his shirt half off his back and his two paws pressed before his chest. "How's about a ig-bay iss-kay?"

"Ugh! Who'd wanna kiss a ugly mug like you got on you!"

Luellen gave him a shove. He grabbed again. She pounded on his back, but he locked his arms about her hips and pressed his face into her stomach. From the scratching and scraping on the silk of her dress, you'd think he was scouring her cheek with his beard.

"Jeez—" Donny said, and caught his breath.

Reuben was grunting and digging down the front of her dress. A ripping sound. A white breast slipped out, the nipple big and black as a bull's-eye. He reached for it with his lips.

"—zuss," Donny said, and let out his breath.

Luellen was punching and socking Reuben with all her might. He was pushing her backwards, almost knocking her down; she had to hold on to his shoulders to keep from going over. He kept nuzzling. With a small sound—surprise or protest—she tossed back her head. Her throat rose; for a minute she was all pearly white from her chin to her chest. Then her head swung forward and her hair came switching down, loosened all around him. It hung over his face, his thick neck and hairy back. She dragged it this way and that, shaking it out in ripples from the braids.

In the dim light, her hair was like seaweed sliding on waves.

Reuben had hold of her hips, solid in her girdle, and

as she leaned over him, hands groping, hair dipping, dripping, he was pushing her backwards. His knees thumped and thudded. In this manner—clasped and swaying—they disappeared into the hallway, to the tune of a heavy object bumping downstairs.

Donny had hold of my arm and was pinching it hard. "Jesus Christ," he said. "Jesus Christ," he said.

A screech, a scramble, a shriek. A loud Abarbanel laugh. The bedsprings gave a snicker, and another. And another. You couldn't tell which voice was whose. One harsh, rising in rhythm, as if someone might be yelping Help Help Help. The other more gentle, even plaintive; Boo-jee, fussing and fretting with its feathers, or a pigeon hooting.

It was Reuben.

Tante Malkeh had stopped snoring in mid-note— mid-air. The grass in the headlamps stood erect as the hair on the back of your neck, except where a tire had flattened a streak. From grass, bushes, branches, petals, leaves, heat was rising; soaking up air; sopping it up. There was nothing to breathe. The night was listening to itself, lying in wait; the ripe supine Indiana summer.

Slowly the silence sank in.

Donny's eyes penetrated the dark; the medal gleamed in the links of hair on his chest.

"Esti?"

What if he wanted me to say something? And how should I know, what he wanted me to say?

I waited; scared, wondering.

He shook his head. "On second thought, you know what? Skip it," he said.

THE
OLD
WHEEZE

If there was one thing Mrs. Cheatham liked, it was her privacy; and privacy was one thing she had. That much she could say for getting old. Not that she could say much more; but who expected it to be easy? She kept to herself all she wanted. People didn't notice her, they paid no attention, and they thought that she didn't notice them, either. She knew more about them than they gave her credit for; a whole lot more than they knew about her.

Take her first name. Did anyone care if she owned one? Well, she did: LaVonne. It had been a while since she heard it. A cousin back in Birmingham, a brother in Detroit, were just about the last ones left to call her by name. (At the clinic she went to for her high blood pressure, they LaVonned her to death; but that didn't count, she didn't mean *familiar.*) And if anyone had told her she would ever miss her sister, that know-it-all, bossing her around in a high-strung, high-tone voice! —LaVonne, why don't you this? and LaVonne, how come you that? —A funny thing about the voice; it was short and sharp, as sudden as a laugh, and every now and then Mrs. Cheatham could have sworn her sister was still talking. There were days when the aches and pains didn't bother her near as much; it took some getting used to, losing your own name.

You wouldn't think a little thing like that.

She was tall, spare, with a small yellow face—like an onion, she thought—and crinkly white hair; the same glittering edge as her glasses. The lenses were thick, telescopically thick, and from the outside you couldn't see anything moving: her eyes poked and peeped. It made her look cautious. And she was, she had to be. Shrugging, stowing herself into her coat, buttoning up with deft fingers, she might have been girding up—gathering her wits about her; every bit as strict as with her small charges. The little boy stood close, within her territory, seeking her protection, but listening to the sound of rising footsteps, looking out between the bars of the stair rail.

All the way up the stairs came smells of suppers getting cooked, fat spatting in frying pans; voices raised over noisy water pipes and Sunday TV. Wet galoshes leaned outside doors.

There it was, the glove on the rail; the dark hair splashed with snowflakes. His mother stopped and looked up, stamping her boots, shaking herself out; sprinkling and scattering like a wet friendly dog. Her earrings tinkled, bunches of coins at her cheeks.

"Oh? You're alone?" Mrs. Cheatham put out her head, as if expecting to see someone else. "No one to drive me home then? In this snow and all?"

"It's all right, Mrs. Cheatham, please don't worry. My friend is waiting outside. He'll drive you home."

"If not, I'm entitled to my cab fare, you know," the old woman went on, still talking and peering into the stairwell. The light was out on the landing below. "But try and find a cab on a night like this."

She was only trying to put off the worst, by forever suspecting it. She had peeped round the corner—looked both ways—seen it coming.

"You had a nice time, I hope?"

"Oh yes, thank you. Very nice." Sydney noticed that her jaws ached from smiling so much. They had cracked with the effort. Maybe she hadn't had such a nice time.

"Markie? What're you waiting for? Where's Mommy's hug? How about a big kiss?" She stooped and spread her arms and caught the child to her. He felt the outdoors stiff on her face.

They looked alike; the same high color, curly black hair, deep, dark-fringed eyes. Her cheeks were bright and eager with cold, his with emotion.

"My my my, but that child favors you. He's as pretty as he could be. And I'm not just saying it, either. Why you don't try and get him on television—"

Mrs. Cheatham saw boys and girls on the advertising commercials all the time, and she had yet to see one half as cute as Mark. She supposed everyone must tell his mother that. And he was a good boy too. "Weren't you, Mark? Ask him if he didn't eat his dinner right down. And didn't you take a nice long nap for me? Two whole hours. Quiet as a mouse."

Two hours. Now how would Sydney get him to sleep? Leo would be coming back as soon as he had dropped the sitter off, and he thought that the child would be in bed.

She looked impressed. "I can never get him to nap."

"He naps for me," Mrs. Cheatham said. "You'd be surprised. They nap for me."

The two women beamed at the little boy, as if that was all he was really for; a vessel to be filled, stuffed with food and sleep, under the snaps and straps of his corduroys. His face had the sober glow of the child just washed.

Sydney opened her purse; Mrs. Cheatham pulled back her sleeve to look at her watch. A Mickey Mouse watch; a bold black and white face; one of her few ingratiating tricks and ways. "Uh-oh, guess what Mickey says now," she'd say, pressing the back of her wrist to her ear—trying to hear. "Tsk tsk tsk, time to go to bed." She would put her wrist to the child's ear too; they liked to listen to ticking. Her eyes ticked inside glasses thick as watchcases. And she knew how it felt, hating to go to bed, always afraid to miss something.

Not that she didn't know what time it was; she had checked the minute she heard the buzzer. And she liked to be paid in small bills and change, so she could hide her money here and there, in linings, waistbands, pockets sewn about her person. In her neighborhood, old people were held up by roving gangs—a war of youth against age. The thieves swiped their blurred smeary glasses, or smashed them for spite; forced the old people to empty their pockets and purses, their shopping bags and even their shoes; left them to stand on cold sidewalks in stocking feet.

"And no chance to hide the holes in the heels and toes then," the old woman said. "Youth. That's what they call them in the papers, you know. I can remember when that was a nice word. Such a sweet sound to it. Youth."

She had a slight tremor of the head; it shook with the effort to steady itself. She tucked and knotted her scarf under her chin, and her face got smaller, more cautious and peeping than ever. "Oh those liberals," she said. "Grrr. They make me so mad. I just wish I could get my hands on one of them."

She believed that the liberals were to blame for what she called *conditions.*

"Mark? Where is that Mark? Where'd he get to? What's he up to now?" Mrs. Cheatham looked all about her, as if she had lost something. Her brows rounded and wrinkled over the smooth circles of her glasses. "Don't I get a goodbye from him?"

Mark hadn't gone anywhere, of course; he was standing right there, right in front of her, inside the open doorway; grinning up foolishly—not sure she was fooling. The double row of dark lashes made his glance shy, like his mother's.

"Make bye-bye, Markie," Sydney whispered, taking hold of his arm, paddling it up and down. His hand opened and squeezed.

"That's better. Goodbye, Mark. —And you won't forget now, will you? Next time you need a sitter and call the Agency, you'll be sure and ask for me by name?"

She had started down the stairs, her shopping bag on her arm, her head leaning out—looking sharp—someone trying to cross a busy street; her shins lumpy in galoshes and elastic stockings. Loaded down like this— scarf, sweaters, bagging pockets—she seemed all at once to be harnessed to her own body; standing between her long arms and thin shanks like a horse in shafts.

"Be careful," Sydney called after her, fearful for her. "You want to watch out for that bottom step. The carpet's loose."

As if Mrs. Cheatham didn't know.

Mrs. Cheatham went into people's houses,
she knew what their lives were like. She saw the way they
looked when they went out the door, all dressed up, at
their best, smiling in the mirror, wanting to be seen.
And she saw what they left behind them—sloppy bath-
rooms, unmade beds, dishes in the sink. She saw the
way their children were brought up. Was it their fault
if they didn't get raised right, poor things? Didn't know
enough to say Yes, Ma'am and No, Thank You, let alone
Grace or the Lord's Prayer or even so much as a Now-I-
Lay-Me.

And didn't her hands itch, once in a while, to pitch
into that mess? Wash dishes, make beds, scour a little
here, dust a little there. It was a strong temptation. But
if she did, and if they ever found out about it at the
Agency, she could get in plenty of hot water. That
would be Housekeeping—nothing but their fancy name
for day work—and they charged extra. She wasn't getting paid for it.

And, once in a while, didn't she wish that those children were hers? The smart-alecky ones; the ones that
paid no mind and sassed right back. Only for a minute
or two was all, long enough so she could get her hands
on them. A good licking, one quick smart smack might
do. The best thing that ever happened, for all you know.
Save the parents a lot of heartache later on, not to
mention a fortune in doctor bills. Leave it to white folks.
What wouldn't they think up next? Mrs. Cheatham
knew all about them and their doctors.

All the same, she had never laid a hand on another woman's child and she never would. It was strictly against her personal principles. That was her policy. And besides, she wasn't getting paid to do that, either.

Mrs. Cheatham went into people's houses, she knew what their lives were like. And she didn't need to be told there was something wrong here. Not that it was any of her business, but there sat that man again, waiting in his car; the same man who drove her home whenever she looked after Mark. The one Mark's mother called her *friend.* That was as might be; but anyone could see, friend or no friend, he was not The Man for Her. He was Old Enough to Be Her Father. And that wasn't all. Mrs. Cheatham wouldn't be a bit surprised but what he was a Married Man too.

He was leaning across the passenger seat to open the door for her.

The motor was running, taillights staining the smoke and snow red. The windshield wipers chased back and forth, wet raggedy flakes flopping against the glass, flowing upward in streams. A rattling rusty old clunker of a car; a regular eyesore; the name of the make was on the tip of her tongue. It would come to her in a minute.

"Well, Missus C.? How about it? What's your opinion? Think we're in for some snow?"

The old woman pressed her lips together and turned down the corners of her mouth. She supposed that this must be one of his jokes. She wasn't used to having people joke with her—teasing or pleasing, either way (and she guessed he meant a little of both)—or calling her Missus C., and she wasn't sure how she liked it. So she settled herself down, like this—her gloves perched on her shopping bag, her shopping bag perched on her knees, her lips perched on her face.

It could have been a frown, it could have been a smile.

"If worse comes to worst, Mister Warshaw," she said.

"If worse comes to worst! I like that!" He gave a squawk; that was his laugh. "Serves me right. I give up, you win. But what a cynic you are. Did anyone ever tell you that? Missus C., you surprise me. You're a *cynic qua non.*"

Oh-oh. There he went again. Laughing his head off. What did that mean? Was he laughing at her? Had she said something funny? Did he want her to laugh too? That cracked squawking laugh and winded voice didn't go with the rest; sounded strange, coming out of him.

He was a fine-looking man, and about as big as they come. There was scarcely room for him behind the wheel, what with his laugh and his chest and his fur-lined lapels. His great big balding head was fur-trimmed too; thick patches of white over his ears, thick black patches of eyebrows and mustache. His nose reminded her of the king or jack on a deck of cards, and his eyes were soft and glossy, almost black. Italians and Jews had eyes like that. Mrs. Cheatham knew Italians and Jews, had lived among them much of her life, and she would have said Italian—because your Italians are flashier—if not for the name. And the way he laughed at his jokes. Had to, most likely; or else how was anyone to know that he meant to be funny?

Well, let him. Men, men—they had to be humored.

She ought to know. Her father had been a man, and so had Mr. Cheatham.

And she didn't like to hurt his feelings; he was driving her home.

Lately Mrs. Cheatham had been having a dream.

She was riding on a streetcar, one of those old-fashioned red cars with the yellow cane seats and the conductor leaning way out over the side, yanking on the bell for all he was worth. (She liked to hear that clanging at night, never knew where it was coming from or where it was going.) They hadn't had cars like that on the lines in she didn't know how long. No wires, no tracks, the very bricks they were laid in all tarred over. Anyway, there she was, riding along; and the next thing you know, she had missed her stop. Gone way past—way out —somewhere she had never been. All the way to the end of the line.

The car stopped. The motor died. The lights went black.

The wind blew them out.

When the old woman woke up—she had to get up more than once now, anyhow—in the night, when she woke up, she didn't feel relieved any; the way you feel when you wake up from a bad dream. And she knew why. Because what she felt in her dream was what she felt night after night, making her way to her flat through the corridors, elevators, half-lit hallways—the empty innards of her building.

She felt safe enough behind her own door, with its bolts and chains, but she dreaded the times of coming and going.

It wasn't the projects, or low-cost housing for the elderly, or one of those apartment hotels with old peo-

ple set out in the lobby like Salvation Army chairs, and
Mrs. Cheatham was proud of that. When Mr. Cheatham
was alive, she had had her own house and yard, and had
kept rabbits out back; and if he hadn't got sick—he had
sugar—she'd be keeping them still. No, this was a real
regular apartment building, with all sorts of people in
it, free to come and go. Too many sorts, that was the
trouble. Drunks, bums, riffraff, white trash. And if those
two girls that had just moved in on the second floor
weren't what-she-thought-they-were, then Mrs. Cheatham would just like to know what was.

You'd never know it now—nothing left to the lobby
but paint and linoleum—but it had been a fancy address
once upon a time. Or so other tenants said; she was only
taking their word for it. Old Jewish ladies, in fur coats
that had seen better days, with holes cut in their shoes
so their bad feet could stick out. Still, they were nice
enough to say hello in the elevator. The elevator! The
worst of all! Leaking and clattering like a bucket lowered down a well. She hated to take it—you never knew
who might get in—but she had six flights to go. It had
got so she was even afraid of black boys now; she was
already afraid of white ones. Some days she didn't know
what to be afraid of first.

And there was another thing. The smell. She thought
for sure it was gas escaping and called the Company;
but they said they had sent a man out and found nothing. Mrs. Cheatham knew leaking gas when she smelled
it. What was it then? Where was it coming from? What
was leaking, if it wasn't gas?

She couldn't say anything to this man, though. Say
she was afraid to set foot inside her own building? What
did he know about it? What would he think? And he was

nice about seeing her home. He apologized for not helping her in and out of the car—he had a bum leg, he said, though to tell the truth Mrs. Cheatham couldn't see what was wrong with it—and he made a point of waiting out front when he dropped her off, watching to make sure she got in all right. The vestibule was brightly lit; fluorescent tubes, shiny paint, tin mailboxes. Too bright; even the lights winced.

Some of these men. The way they just sat there, in their overcoats, humming through their teeth, impatient for the stoplights to go from red to green; smelling of cigarettes and meat grease and that perfume stuff they slapped on their cheeks. And whatever it was they had been drinking too much of. Lord knows she didn't get to pick and choose. And then the ones who had nothing better to do than to start sneaking looks at her. As if she didn't know very well she talked to herself. She had to talk to someone, didn't she? And someone had to talk to her?

You'd think they never laid eyes on an old cottonhead colored lady before.

The windshield wipers were sliding and swiping; through wet steamy glass the colors of traffic lights streaked and blurred, runny as paint.

"I hope you had a nice time?" she said.

"Who? Me?"

He reared back his head and raised up his brows to have a look at her; lip stiff with mustache, whiskers white as shaving soap alongside his ears. "Who, me? You mean the ballet? Just between you and me, and please don't tell anybody I said so, but I thought it stunk. Junk! Bunk! Pas de Do, Pas de Don't. But what do *I* know? I don't go in for that sort of thing. The

ladies, they're the ones. They like to fancy themselves
up there hopping around, dressed in nothing but tal-
cum powder and cheesecloth."

"Was it a stage show, then?"

Sometimes Mrs. Cheatham couldn't make heads or
tails, the way he talked; and all his grinning at his jokes.
(If that is what they were; she liked to give people the
benefit of the doubt.) Well, she'd laugh too—if she was
a man, and white, and had his chances. She had wondered what he did for a living. A lawyer? A politician?
Some kind of crook? Mark's mother said he was a critic.
So Mrs. Cheatham still couldn't have told you what he
did.

"I didn't know you went to a real live stage show."

"Stage show? Maybe. Live? I don't know. It was a
benefit matinee, only don't ask me whose. So-so-ciety.
But the Superstar, now he was something to see. What
a chest he had! Spangled with ribs! Striding around,
showing off all those bulges in his tights. A regular lion
tamer; all he needed was a whip and a chair. Nope.
Nope. Don't worry, Missus C., you didn't miss a thing.
Take it from me. An act like that would never make the
Regal."

"The Regal, did you say? You don't mean the Regal
Theater?"

"Oho, don't I? I sure do. And why not? I'd like to
know. I've been around a while too. I'm no kid, either."

"I wouldn't say that, Mister Warshaw. You're not that
old."

Another squawk. Now what? Head on, he had a blank
space right between his eyes. She wished he wouldn't
keep looking at her—not while he was driving.

Mrs. Cheatham knew she shouldn't have said *that* old,

but she didn't feel like taking it back. Old wasn't what she meant, anyhow; old had nothing to do with it. And he knew it.

The Regal. The Regal. She hadn't thought of it in years. Mr. Cheatham used to take her on their anniversary; the most splendid place you ever saw in your life. Worth going just to stand in the lobby and stare, never mind the movies and the stage shows. The carpets, the curtains, the chandeliers—if she didn't know better, she would have said they were *ice*. And the crowds, dressed fit to kill. She wore her hat with the veil, her fox-fur collar, and the gardenia corsage Mr. Cheatham bought from the fat lady under the El tracks. Why didn't they sell flowers under the El anymore? You could buy plastic plants in the dime store and supermarket, and around the holidays, real ones; but never gardenias, real or not. And not even plastic flowers had such green leaves.

Mr. Cheatham had been a strong solid-built man, on the short side; dress-up clothes looked too tight on him, as if he might start popping buttons. She could see his sharp white collar, the straight line of his haircut, and, in between, the black bulge of his neck. That was how she thought of him now; from the back. It bothered her; she worried she might not know him right off, in case she saw him coming.

It was the sugar. First it crippled, then it killed him.

"Well, well, well. The Regal. That goes back, doesn't it? That brings back the memories. They can keep their ballets and their matinees; me, I'll take the Regal any day. That's what I call a real live stage show! These guys wouldn't stand a chance. No sir, not on your life. —And I suppose it's been closed up for years by now?"

"I don't rightly know, Mister Warshaw. I really couldn't say."

Yes, closed up. Boarded up. Scribbled up. Smashed up. The walls faded and peeling and stripped like bill-boards. She hated to think what went on behind them; bad enough what went on out front. And nothing, not a name, not a letter, on the marquee. The best black performers in the U.S.A. had played the Regal; and at the Regal they had played to their own.

There were plenty of places for white folks to go. Why did they have to pick on the Regal? Who asked them? Who wanted them? It made her feel the way she felt when they caught her talking to herself. Not that she cared what they thought; but she didn't like the sneak-ing sidewise glances, the funny looks on their faces. Why couldn't they keep their white noses out of it? Why couldn't they mind their own white business?

And here he was, telling her all about it; all the acts he had seen, and amateur nights, and how he used to go all the time, way back when, in his university days. (Did he mean the one on the South Side, where they had those Communists and kidnappers?) Laughing and smiling and showing off all the bridgework in his teeth. He wasn't the only one. Mrs. Cheatham had bridgework of her own. But she at least had sense enough to keep her mouth shut and keep it to herself. What people don't know won't hurt them.

Him. Telling her. About the Regal.

All at once it came to her—she didn't know how she knew, but she knew—he must be one of those liberals. A liberal, that's what he was! That explained it. She stared straight at him, eyes drilling in her glasses; eyes in peepholes. She'd never seen a liberal before. Not this close. Not that she knew of.

So that's what they were like.

Why someone didn't get hold of that girl and talk some sense into her! Mrs. Cheatham would have, she could guarantee, if it was one of hers. A good talking-to was what was needed. Find herself some nice young man who made a steady living and was willing to look after her and her little boy. As pretty as she was, it should be no trouble. (Those big eyes and blushing cheeks; she looked almost *ashamed* to be so pretty.) And Mark was such a good little boy. Too good; it didn't seem natural. When Mrs. Cheatham peeked in on him after she got him to bed she saw he was lying awake, for the longest time, the covers moving up and down over his chest and his eyes blinking and shining. Still Waters Run Deep. She felt his face to see did he have a temperature, his cheeks were so flushed and his eyes so serious.

And you can be sure the man would be heading straight back there—soon as he got rid of her; Mrs. Cheatham didn't pretend not to know what everybody knew. But she didn't need to think about such goings-on, either. All she wanted to think about was getting home, to her own flat, where it was neat and clean and she knew where everything was, which was right where she had put it! Right where it belonged! One lamp was left burning, she allowed herself that extra; she did hate to come home to the dark. She had noticed a hole in her glove when she was pulling it on; she hoped she would remember to sew it up. (At the thought of the small task, the thimble flashing on her fingertip, the precise eager pricking of the needle, her eyes pricked and flashed.) First, she would fix herself a cup of tea. The water drumming in the kettle; the pop of the gas when it sucked up the match. The blue teeth of flame. And while she was waiting for the water to boil, she would rub her legs. They ached so from the damp and cold; no rubbing could reach them. Still, it was a comfort— stroking, talking to them, as she might stroke and pet and soothe a dog or cat, some old, once-serviceable companion:

There, there, LaVonne. There, that's all right.

She looked up, lips prim; wondering if she had spoken aloud.

Brakes and tires were skidding and squealing—scolding voices. —How are you today, LaVonne? Now, LaVonne, this will stick a bit. LaVonne, LaVonne, why haven't you been taking your medicine? Sometimes she just wanted to look around and see who this LaVonne was they kept talking to, at the clinic. They got so many foreigners; maybe they didn't know she was born right here and could speak plain English. There was one wrinkled soul who couldn't even say the name of her own complaint! Had it written down on a piece of paper, so she could ask everyone else to read it out for her.

Maybe it made her feel important; it was sure a mighty long name.

"Don't you worry, Missus C. We'll get you there. Safe and sound. This old buggy may not look so hot and she may not sound so hot. But she's solid as a tank. She's got enough scrap iron."

He pounded the wheel from habit or affection; leaning across it, wiping off the glass with his glove. His

keen kind eyes glanced at the old woman; her tight
yellow face, her head trembling and tucked into her
scarf, her lips compressed as if they were biting off
thread.

Snow was swirling, giddy in the headlamps, the light
driving it all before them—threshing it like white grain.

Winter. The worst humiliation of all. The cold, the
icy streets, the early dark. The blasts in the face. The
sneak thief, the mugger in the hall, the knife in the ribs.
Winter.

And oh yes, LaVonne. Don't you go and forget about
that glove.

As soon as Mrs. Cheatham had gone, and
she took Mark inside, Sydney went around opening windows and putting out lights. The old woman made a
practice of shutting and bolting every window in the
flat, and turning on all the lights; then she sat herself
down with her newspapers and her knitting and whatever else it was she kept in that shopping bag of hers,
and made herself at home. And when she left, it was as
if she had taken something with her. The place looked
emptier than ever; evacuated. The four walls sprang up
with powers of their own.

Sydney took off her things as she went along, tossing
her scarf here, throwing her gloves there, dropping her
coat on the sofa bed; leaning her face over the lamps.
She pinched dead leaves off the wandering Jew. (Sydney
never felt sure if she was giving her plants too much

water or too little, so she did each by turns.) Her movements were aimless and abrupt, her earrings plunging
at her cheeks; her boots struck the floor with a pound-
ing rhythm. Mark trotted after his mother, trying to
keep up with her, to look into her face—seeking to
reassure himself that she was there, and to remind her
of his own existence.

Mark went to nursery school; he was used to being
away from his mother. Or, if not used to it—how could
he ever get used to it?—he didn't question it. It was a
part of life, one of its conditions; a sensation that per-
vaded life, like being hungry or sleepy or cold. He
didn't ask *why*. But this was different. It was different
because his mother was different. He had learned to
know the signs, and here was one of them: the sound
of her high heels driving into the floor.

The sound she made when she was getting ready to
go out.

Mark would follow her then as he was following her
now, his face tipped up—tilted toward her—as if to
catch and hold her smile, her glance. She would lean
into the mirror over the sink, turning her cheeks this
way and that, smearing things round her eyes with her
pretty pointy fingers. Under the light, she brought her
face closer and closer, looking into it as anxiously as he
was; looking for something in it too. She touched behind her ears, her neck, her elbows, her wrists; and the
more she touched, the stronger she smelled.

He could feel the sting in the back of his throat.

By now Mark would be expecting the worst—and the
worst would come. The sound of the buzzer. Her footsteps quickened; so did his. —But not quick enough.
His mother hoisting her coat over her arm, stooping to

plant a sticky kiss half on his mouth, half on his chin. When she shut her eyes he saw slivers of green on her lids. He knew for certain that she was going away, going without him, and it must be his fault that she was leaving him.

But why? What had he done?

Her smell stayed on him after she was gone.

Most times Mrs. Cheatham came at night, when it was dark; she put Mark into his pajamas and then to bed. She left the door open a crack so that a bar of light fell across the floor and bent and went climbing up the wall. Noises came from the street; lights teetered over the ceiling. He could feel his eyes swimming in the dark.

When Mark woke, it would be daylight, and he would run first thing to the other room, where his mother slept, to make sure that everything was all right; as it should be. He liked best the way she smelled these mornings, her cheek against the pillow, the pillow soft and scented as her cheek. He would put a finger on her eyelid and lift. A circle staring in the midst of white. Then there were two.

She laughed when he kissed her face again and again.

"Hey. What's got into you? You kiss-bug you. What's the big idea? Stop. Enough."

The truth is, Mark didn't care for kissing or getting kissed. It was noisy and wet and made him want to wipe his face. Only he had to wait until no one was looking, and by then it was too late. What he wanted—all he wanted—was to smell his mother's cheek. But kissing was what grownups liked and needed. So he would kiss and kiss, making loud smacking noises; just so he could sniff away, in secret.

But today when his mother went away and left him it

was still light out, and Mark didn't know what to think.

Maybe that meant she was coming right back? Again and again he heard her step rising up the stairs. His heart rose under his buckles and straps.

He ran straight to Mrs. Cheatham and stood beside her chair, waiting for her to hear it too.

Mark couldn't interrupt her, the way he could interrupt his mother. Her face was tucked in and tight under her snug white hair. He waited, raising submissive eyes to her: expecting her to hear—willing her to.

"Yes, Mark? What is it now, son?"

The glasses lifted and lighted on him.

The radiators sizzled and fell silent.

The footsteps went away.

Whenever he was apart from his mother, Mark took his nap without any fuss. At nursery school, along with rows of other children, he rolled out his rug on the cracked linoleum (it had a yellowish gloss, like Mrs. Cheatham's face and fingers, but smelled *pink*) and shut his eyes. Apart from his mother, he lost interest in being awake or even alive. Maybe when he woke up, she would be back.

But when Mark woke, it wasn't morning and it wasn't night; the light was pale and wrinkled as the sheets on his bed. He felt cold, as if he had wet them. Something was falling past the window. He couldn't see out, but he stood and watched it fall, getting darker, getting darker. It was closest to his mother; she was somewhere out there. Darkness was falling; he couldn't see where.

Mark had missed his mother terribly; breathing was missing her. Missing her was his life. Nothing could make up for it now—not even her.

"C'mere, Markie. I want to show you something."

His mother was leaning out the window, her earrings tinkling at her cheeks—something breaking far away. Her hair was cropped and curly, like his, revealing the shape of her head, the nape of her neck. He saw the glimmer of green on her lids, her eyes shimmering on the verge of black lashes, and he thought for a minute she might be crying.

The thought stiffened and stifled him. Could a *mother* cry?

"Upsy-daisy. There. Now what do you think of *that?*"

She hoisted him to her hip, his cheek to her cheek. They had a view of brick; of flat gravelled roofs, smoke-stacks, chimneys. Smoke was rising, clumps of it; smoke-shrubbery, smoke-bushes, smoke-trees. Wherever there were lights, there were streaks. The air was flickering. The glass was cold. The chill seemed a property of it, like the darkness.

"That's snow, Markie. Can you say snooh?"

"—nooh!"

"That's right. Good for you. Snooh."

Under the streetlamps the stuff was spinning, spinning—soft cocoons.

His mother began to recite, touching her nose to his, rounding her eyes and her lips:

> *"The North Wind doth blow*
> *And we shall have snow*
> *And what will poor Robin do then?"*

Her eyes were so close there was only one of them now.

It winked.

. . .

"So, you stinker," his mother said. "What do I hear? So you decided to sleep all day?" A hug, a kiss; she put Mark down. "What am I supposed to do with you now?"

She plopped onto the couch and kicked off her boots, forcing the heel of one with the toe of the other. They fell with soft blows. And her footsteps were more famil-iar now—slippery, whispering to him—in her stocking feet.

Mark was neater and cleaner than Syd-ney, his own mother, was used to seeing him. His face scrubbed bare—polished to a shine—gleaming on him like a new identity. And he seemed to know it. He looked the way he did when he sat in the barber's chair, eyes deep and cheeks bright, spying on himself above the striped sheet in the mirror. Whenever he had been with Mrs. Cheatham, he seemed sobered, more self-conscious; to have grown older—grown up—grown apart.

Sydney couldn't blame him; she felt intimidated her-self by Mrs. Cheatham—the old woman's skin the color of laundry soap, her lips (but barely) confining her opinions. For Mrs. Cheatham, she got the idea, there was good and bad—right and wrong—and if you weren't one, you were the other. But this was good for Mark, Sydney believed, and good for her; an antidote to her own erratic ways. Because what did she know about being a *mother?*

Love him? Of course she loved him. What a question!

She loved him rashly, at times frantically—squeezing him to her as if he were her life, her breath, and she could scarcely catch him. Still, in her heart of hearts, she suspected that almost anyone would be better at her job, more qualified, than she was. By this she meant: someone else would see to it that he took his nap regularly, and got to bed on time; that he ate what was on his plate; that he was washed and combed—as spick-and-span as he was now—and that his clothes were fresh from the wash. (Sydney had to blush when she thought of all the times when she needed to go fishing, among soiled clothes in a smelly laundry bag, to find something to wear.)

She had her doubts about his nursery school as well, but there was nothing else as close and nothing at all she could afford. Mornings, when she dropped him off at the gravelled playground, her heart sank. Where were the swings? the slides? the teeter-totters? It was nothing but a parking lot! And all the children shivering outside—chastised with cold—like puppets in their peaked hoods and dangling mitten strings. All those chapped cheeks and runny noses. Mark—her child—wasn't one of them. But her heart sank more when she came to pick him up. In that first instant, when she saw his face—before she knew it was his face, his and no other—he looked the same as all the rest. She saw how small and helpless he really was.

They lived in the neighborhood of a reputable university. It was not particularly cheap or safe or convenient; certainly not clean. Not even picturesque. Squat solid close-stacked three-flats, or deep courtyard buildings; dark brown or scaly red or mustard yellow brick; aqueduct arches, wrought-iron rails, slabs of cement. Roughnecked grass pushed through sidewalks, curbstones, pop-top tabs, bottle caps, broken glass. There was variety in the streets; dark-skinned foreign students, Indian women sandalled and sari-ed, Sikhs in gauzy turbans of confectionery colors, spun sugar; but there was little vitality. The main street was being upgraded, renovated, and few of the usual commercial establishments remained. —A Mom & Pop grocery of the sort where the pop bottles came dripping wet from an ice cooler, and the corpses of last season's flies could be viewed—fuzzy shadows—in the globe of the light fixture. A liquor store; a dry cleaner; a pharmacy with its discouraging display of rubber objects, bedpans, plaster limbs, and elastic bandages; a bakery where the same scalloped cardboard wedding cakes sat year in and year out on the same scalloped paper doilies. —But most of these old-fashioned shops, with their old-fashioned services and skills, had moved on. The new ones were of brick and butcher block and stained glass, and narrow-eyed thick-skinned cats snoozed in their fern-steamy windows. "First the butcher and the baker," as Leo Warshaw put it, "and now we get the candlestick maker." Arts and crafts. Potters. Weavers. Health food; head shops; tie-dyed T-shirts and macrame plant holders; scented balls of soap kneaded by hand. Bubbling water. Bins and barrels of snapping-eyed coffee beans.

Also: soaped-up storefronts; tattoo parlors; porno peep shows; gypsy fortune tellers behind curtains and beads; pinball machines blasting the street with sounds of combat, strafing, bombing, and blitz. The neighborhood was not upward-mobile, it was not downward-mobile. It was just mobile. Even the trash looked transient: flapping against fences, scratching in gutters.

Pigeons flew up like gritty winds, gusts of newspapers, printed scraps for wings.

Through it all blew keen clean fortifying breezes; these streets ran close to the lake—a hidden mirror flashing signals of light. It was large as a sea. The city lay along its shining curve as in the palm of a hand, a commotion of stone, metal, haze and glass—a boundary not so much in space as in time.

Sydney worked at the university and was taking courses, tuition-free, but outside classes she rarely crossed paths with other students, and when she did it was only in the supermarket, the laundromat. Notices were posted on bulletin boards. Flats to share. Used skis/tennis rackets/ten-speed bikes for sale. Rides offered to distant cities. Lectures/concerts/silent films. Marches, vigils, rallies, protests. Sydney knew that she was not political, but when she saw these mimeographed announcements, with their inked and blotted drawings—manacled fists, machetes—she reminded herself that she had always meant to be.

She had never picked out a life for herself and so she thought that all were still available.

Sydney was only a few years older than these college girls, but it seemed to her that they were an age she had never been. Had she ever had those years?—nineteen? twenty? twenty-one? Rooming in dormitories, pledging sororities, sending out for pizza at two in the morning? —She folded Mark's socks and shirts and footed pajamas (he was dressing himself now and put things inside out and backward, the labels up front where he thought they belonged). Clothes thrashed in washers, whirled in dryers. In portholed windows, bras, jeans, panty hose were flaunted and flung. Stripes, rags, colored flags—symbols, she thought, of her drudgery and their freedom.

Sydney wondered about other people's lives.

No one had been surprised when Sydney married so young, right out of high school, at a time when her friends were going off to college; that had been expected, she had been the Beauty. She had worked to put her husband through school, and when her friends were taking their first jobs (most got teaching certificates), she had had Mark. And now that these old friends were marrying, buying houses, starting families (as they had meant to do, all along)—here she was; working at the same old jobs, going to school; back where she started. No one was surprised by that, either. It was a satisfaction of sorts; not malicious, not even personal. So she hadn't done very well for herself, had she, in spite of her looks? A lot she had to show for it now. —The pretty-pretty eyes, the pink-and-white cheeks, the lustrous lashes which actually seemed to caress them. She might have been embarrassed by her looks, blushing for them; trying to subdue them with her downcast glances—hiding the light of her eyes. That made her prettier than ever.

The marriage had not been happy, and not really, Sydney felt, a marriage. Not that she knew what a marriage really was; but she was sure there ought to be more to it than that. She didn't miss her former husband (Sydney didn't care for the term "ex"; it suggested something acquired rather than lost, some status she could not connect with herself; but she did have to admit it was a lot easier to say). She didn't miss him, and she was never as lonely now as she had been with him; though often she was more frightened. And yet in that respect also; that there was nothing much to be sorry about, nothing special to regret; no very great loss because there had been so little to lose—she felt short-changed. She would rather have regrets.

Sydney lived as she always had, in a state of expectation; from one event to the next; waiting for something to happen, for her life to change, for better or worse. Now her expectations centered on Leo Warshaw. How could she help it? At intermission this afternoon there had been a champagne reception in the lobby. Behind the bar, two waiters were filling glasses as on an assembly line; two pairs of red-gartered sleeves and brassy cuff links; two red vests and ruffled shirtfronts. They moved past rows of glass, bottles tilted in each hand, pouring so fast there wasn't time to right them; they kept on spilling—necks gushing, glasses splashing, bubbles washing down the bar. A suds of champagne.

The glasses were snatched up as quickly as they were filled.

Swilling, Sydney thought. We are *swilling* champagne.

People kept rushing up to say hello; Leo standing, as always, a head above the crowd. (There was something about his head, chest, shoulders—but especially his head, the hair erect in the back—that made him seem to rise and swell from his body: a jinni from a bottle.) Sydney couldn't catch any names, and no one caught hers—she couldn't hear it herself—but it didn't matter. Already they were on the lookout for other faces, others to see and be seen by, rushing off to be discovered and hailed by someone else.

The very chandeliers were buzzing, hives of crystal and brass.

Leo leaned down, his mouth and mustache behind his hand. "Well, here's your great world for you. Terra Incognito. I just hope you're satisfied."

Sydney laughed; it made her cheeks hurt. She didn't always like Leo's jokes, she didn't always get them; but she always laughed.

With her neighbors, Sydney shared a dim hallway and back porch; the garbage cans and dented lids, the clotheslines squawking on pulleys. Their underwear jiggled in wooden clothespins. The wife wore plastic hair curlers and had a chin as long as your foot; the two little boys fought; once a week the father played ball with them in the alley, his belly sloping and slumping over his belt buckle. —A beer belly; empty cans gleamed in the garbage. He yelled at the kids, showing off, and socked the ball into his glove. And yet when she saw all of them coming from the supermarket, as they did, every Saturday morning—the entire family unloading bags from the back of the car—Sydney felt what she always felt when she had a glimpse of other families. She didn't know what to call it, a splinter of something; envy, or remorse.

And, running upstairs tonight, she had felt it again. The light was out on the landing. The radiators were hissing and cracking; water blabbing, babbling in drainpipes; wet galoshes leaning outside doors. (*Roosting*, she thought.) The noises, the cooking smells, the wet boots by the doors—the very doors themselves— seemed to hold and withhold some secret. —Wouldn't she ever be in on it?

Sydney wondered about other people's lives and felt that her life was no life at all.

Well, well, well. What's this? What have we here? Mark? Is that Mark?"

The man stood in the doorway, taking it all up, looking out from under the lofty tips of his eyebrows, over his lofty lip. Drops twinkled in his black mustache; his eyes were wet-black and twinkling. There was snow on his shoulders and down the front of his coat, and the hairs on the sides of his face were thick and white too.

He scraped his foot and slapped his big gloves together.

"Well, Mark? How d'ya do?" The man put out his hand.

Mark looked at the hand and up at the man, not sure what was coming or what was expected of him. "Say hel-lo," his mother whispered, taking Mark's hand, its fat cluster of fingers and puddles of dimples. "Say how do you do?"

She held the hand out, offering and urging. "Shake, Markie. Shake hands."

Mark took back his hand.

He snatched it back, hiding it behind him, wiping it possessively on the seat of his pants. That was plainly his intention—to take back what belonged to him.

"Maaarkie!"

"Shh. Never mind, don't yell at him. He sure takes after you, doesn't he?"

"He's not used to you," Sydney said.

Leo smiled to himself. She was *apologizing;* she

thought his feelings might be hurt. She knew what people said about children and dogs. Leo had had his share
of both, let others have theirs, but he'd just as soon they
didn't take a shine to him, and he didn't put much stock
in their opinions. Winks, chuckles, pats on the head,
foolish grins, were not his line. What to say to such
small, expectant, excitable creatures? Their open
mouths and big eyes?

He was surprised to see the boy up; usually Sydney
kept him hidden, well out of sight; old-world of her. It
reminded Leo of his mother, with her distracted ways
and straying hair (coarse, black, crooked as her hairpins
and it wouldn't stay put in spite of them; his eyebrows
were like that now). Five kids in a tiny flat, trying to keep
them out of their father's way. The old man came home
from work in a mood, as fathers will—he was a porter
in the Yards, wore a bloody apron—wanting nothing
but to eat and sleep and read his paper in peace; putting
a child in front of him was waving a flag at a bull. He
wasn't such a big guy (easy to say that, now), but he had
big hands, made for walloping, and no telling when he
might feel like taking a swing. First come first served, he
didn't care who—same way he might swat at flies. That
was one thing about the old man, fair is fair, he didn't
play favorites. Their mother did; Leo was her favorite.
—The times he had peered through keyholes at that
awful figure, his father: asleep, flat on his back; newspapers spread over his face, smudged with inky thumb-
prints, and fluttering—audibly, visibly—with his snores.

Mark had withdrawn his hand, but did not take back
his eyes: they continued to stare and shine.

Leo advanced into the room, stiff leg first, hauling
himself after—all the rest of him—his whole vast expan-

sive self, chest and fur, nose dripping icicles, haywire eyebrows, briny mustache. His rubber heels were tracking in half-circles, horseshoes of slush. He had not forgotten what everyone must know, once upon a time; how ridiculous, or frightening, or both, most grownups seem to a child. (All that saves them from being boring, though.) Monstrosities; almost another species. Their grotesque size, their appalling damages and defects, their terrible authority.

"He's shy at first," Sydney said. "He has to get used to you."

"Shy, my eye. The kid's got it in for me, and I don't blame him. He's *used to* having his mama all to himself."

Now what did he have to say that for! Leo took it for granted that she did not see other men. That happened to be true; all the more reason she didn't like to hear him say it. She knew very well that he saw other women. And there was nothing she could do about it. —It wasn't him and her; it was men and women.

"But, Leo. What happened? Where were you? What took you so long? I was so worried about you. And look at you. You're frozen stiff. And oh, your poor ears."

Sydney blew on her hands and held them over his ears.

"They're so red, you can *see* through them," she said accusingly.

Leo shut his eyes and stuck out his neck, submitting to these attentions with a sheepish expression, his big jowly face between her two hands. His nose grew straight from his forehead; between his eyes, blank flesh. He was so large, so prominent, there was so much of him; and his features were so large and prominent and there seemed to be so many of them; any one of them would have distinguished another face, made the appearance of a lesser man. The eyes, nose, nether lip (it stuck out, not overshadowed by the pelt above it). And still, in the midst of all, most prominent was the space between his upstanding brows and thinning crest. Never had hairline receded so powerfully. He was all forehead—a great glowing reef.

From his shaved cheeks, from his glistening side-burns—from hair and neck—she caught a whiff, some smarting scent. Spiced and sweetened alcohol; hair tonic, aftershave. Gifts, she was sure, from other girl-friends.

"What was it? Not trouble with the car?"

"Nope. Nothing like that." He was vain about the car; an old war horse like himself, he said. "I had to take your baby-sitter upstairs, that's all."

"Mrs. Cheatham? Oh no, what for? She wasn't sick, was she?"

"Her? Sick? Are you kidding? I wish I had her war-ranty. They don't make 'em like that anymore. She's got to be seventy if she's a day, and she can run up six flights without batting an eye. —It almost killed me. No, no, don't you worry about her. —The Powder Was Out."

"Oh all right." Sydney dropped her hands. "Don't tell me then, if you don't want to."

"But I *am* telling you." Leo spread fingers and thumbs on his snow-caked lapels. "Cross my heart and hope to die. The whole place was pitch-dark; no lights, no nothing. I thought there had been a fire—an air-raid drill. (But you wouldn't remember those, would you?) It was creepy. Someone must have blown one helluva fuse. So I had to go in with her and see what was up."

"And a good thing too. I'd hate to think what would

have happened if you weren't there. But you had to walk up? In the dark? With your leg?"

"The halt leading the blind. She had a little flashlight in her shopping bag—one of those things the doctor looks down your throat with, to see if it's sore; and she gave me a candle stump so I could see my way down. And I get outside, and what do I see? Someone has scribbled a sign and stuck it on the door. THE POWDER IS OUT. That's what it says. (Just in case you might not notice.) So it wasn't a total loss. I thought you'd get a kick out of that. The super—if there is a super—must be Puerto Rican."

"Why? I don't get it."

"Because it's Spanish. At least I think it's Spanish." Leo stamped his foot, beating and brushing himself off, whacking his coat with his gloves. "Power—poder—powder. No?"

He turned to shed his coat, she sprang to help him.

"Oh." Oh. Sydney had forgotten. Leo had lived in Mexico, he spoke Spanish. It made her feel glum, reminding her of all the things he had done in his life and she had not done in hers. And probably never would. He was a man, he lived freely, he travelled to other countries and learned foreign languages. He had had experience. How could she ever compete with it? She was jealous of just about everything in his life that wasn't her—and that was just about everything. So now she was jealous of his Spanish.

And think of all the women he had spoken to in Spanish.

Sydney had seen a photograph of Leo Warshaw when he was young, her age; he had published a book of poems. One or two were still anthologized, and this was the picture that went with them. He looked like what he was supposed to be: profile plunging straight forward (a nose like a poniard, he said), hair ploughing straight back (*locks,* Sydney thought). He had been romantically handsome. She saw she would not have cared for him; he would not have cared for her. Too full of himself; the sickle nostrils, the arrogant lip. And he looked touchy; about the last thing anyone would think or say of Leo Warshaw.

Leo didn't care for anthologies; they reminded him of tombstones, he said—the names, the hyphenated dates. "Maybe it ain't poetry, but I never said it was my epitaph." And he didn't care for the picture, either. Once, when she was waiting for him in his office, Sydney had taken it down from the shelf. "Oh, so you're looking at *him?*" Leo said when he came in. He glanced over her shoulder, his head to one side. "Snotty, stuck-up bastard, huh? What do you want to look at *him* for?"

What was conceit, arrogance in the younger man was completeness, accomplishment in Leo. He had plenty of ego, that was no secret; it was his way of sharing himself, his connection with the world. With money he was stingy. That old car he drove, and made so much of (his affection for it yanked and twanged at her string); the ballet tickets today (someone had given them to him, he would never have bought them); his room in an apartment hotel, the folding bed behind a door and a sign red all night outside his window. The sign kept him company, he said; he was a troubled sleeper. True, he was losing his shirt in a divorce case; something about an art collection which had gone up in value—his "hunches and bets"; he was "moving in I. R. Eschelons." But he took to bachelor ways as out of long habit;

washing his socks in the bathroom sink (they shrivelled on radiators); his watch and wallet on the empty wire shelves of the refrigerator, for safekeeping, along with packages of crackers and processed cheese and punched tins of evaporated milk.

With himself he was generous. Most of his jokes were on him, and Sydney had heard most of his jokes. Leo didn't mind repeating himself; old jokes were like old friends, he couldn't snub them. And anyway, they were for his own amusement. He didn't expect anyone else to laugh, and up on the lecture platform seemed surprised, taken aback, when anyone else did. Glancing all about—glaring, really—the caterpillar eyebrows rising in unison; trying to make out what this strange noise was and where it was coming from. —Who dared to interrupt him, in the midst of a good laugh? Reaching inside his jacket for his pen, his papers, he revealed silk linings, labels, monograms—the vestments and splendors of his person.

It was fun to take potshots at such a target; too large to miss—or to do any injury. He was all ego and no vanity, the opposite of her. He kidded her about it:

"Where's your *armour proper?*"

And just now, when he was shedding his coat—presenting his big self-confident back to her, pulling his arms out of his sleeves—he had seemed suddenly covered in armor. All of him. From head to foot. That back, the muscled hump of his shoulders, his cast-iron neck. Yes. Armored. Even his bald brow was muscular—masculine. That was his armor; his maleness, his sex. Spears, crossbows, lances, battle-axes—nothing could touch him. Her anger hurt her so much more than it could ever hurt him.

She hung the wet heavy coat over the door.

"Can I get you anything? Coffee? I was just making some."

"No, thanks. None for me. I think I'll just lie down here and stretch out my leg for a minute."

He was tired. Of course. What was the matter with her? She had almost let it slip past, the opportunity to show her concern for him. She wasted no time showing it now; straightening the pillows, taking off his shoes, hovering about him with swishing skirts and tinkling ears.

The earrings suited her, Leo thought; brash fragile jingling things; they made him think of shoals of fish. — The way they keep darting this way and that, chasing each other, changing direction. So swift, so decisive, such shuddering light and shimmering motion. But why? What for? Where were they off to? Was there any rhyme or reason? All of one mind—and always making it up.

He glanced around the room with regret. He had seen so many like it; half-furnished student dwellings; stringy potted plants, pillows, posters (always the same ones; sunflowers, bullfighters, French cafés); light bulbs in colored paper shades. Still, it lacked certain touches. No empty wine bottles; no candles stuck in raffia, dripping wax all over the place. —Candles Leo couldn't abide, the scented kind least—a morbid combination, incense and wax. But Sydney would not have had candles; candles would be too calculating. She wasn't trying to be Bohemian—she wasn't striving for effect. She lived this way because she hadn't thought about it and didn't know any better; she hadn't consciously chosen it. He doubted if Sydney had ever consciously chosen anything.

She would have been surprised to hear that the way she lived, the way she dressed—the longish skirts and jangling earrings—were a style. It had a name; a history. She would have been pleased—flattered—a kind of discovery; like finding out that we speak in prose. Her version of the Bohemian life was perhaps thirty years out of date, and that was endearing; for him, reminiscent. Leo had always been pursued by women, but he was no different from other men. Being dropped into the midst of a Turkish bath by Ingres—all those turbanned, towel-wrapped, guitar-shaped ladies with the horizontal eyes; that was his idea of pursuit. —Not that he had anything against brains. Brains improved a woman's looks, enlivened her glance. Dullness in a woman was a defect, and a defect in a woman was a crying shame. (He was glad they didn't wear those stockings with seams down the backs anymore; the crooked meandering lines made him feel sorry.) He remembered women as something softer than they were now; these tough acts of theirs were getting too convincing. He thought of the comic-strip image of the caveman; carrying clubs, wearing skins, bopping women over the head and dragging them off by the hair. Well, now there were cavewomen. They ought to wear stripes and spots and stick bones through their chignons (and some of them did). At least no one would be dragging him off by the hair; he didn't have enough of it. Thank God for little things.

He knew that Sydney believed him wise; believed he could see into her, see through her; that he knew all

about her—had guessed her secret—and could tell her,
if he wanted to. Why was he keeping it from her? Leo
didn't lie to himself; that was his attraction for her, for
young women like her; a sort of guru. It just might be
that he cultivated the image; it was his line of business.
And there was something to it. He had a knowledge of
categories, classifications; he could generalize. He
could call things by name. But Sydney knew only par-
ticulars—bits and pieces—her own.

He caught her by the wrist, pulled her to him, plucked
a kiss from her cheek. "Hey? Where're you going? Stick
around, why don't you?" He patted the cushion by his
side.

Sydney blushed and pulled away, flushing with pleasure for the unsolicited attention—flustered at showing
it. "I have to put Mark to bed first," she said. "Markie?
Bedtime, Markie. Do you want to say good night?" She
went toward him, skirts, earrings, swinging, clattering.

Mark's eyes were wide and bright: eyes in keyholes.

His fingers were still tingling, as they had just before
when he heard the buzzer. As if he had touched the
thing that buzzed; as if it had stung him. His mother ran
to the door, and he ran after—his heart racing his feet
—running faster than they could. His mother leaned
over the rail, looking and calling down into the dark.
Someone was coming up the stairs, one at a time. He
heard them bumping; he held on to the bars. Something told him what was coming. Just as when he woke
at night and saw the darkness around his bed, already
stirring, and knew that it would start to move—take
shape—before his very eyes. He held his breath, but
that wouldn't stop it. Nothing would. He couldn't stop
it now. If he shut his eyes, it kept moving. It was as if

he had always known there would be something like
this: this form, this shadow, falling across his path, dark-
ening his life.

The headless coat swayed at the door.

Ｈe felt cold; something rattled at the
open window. A head rested on his chest. He couldn't
tell just now whose head—his arm in pale shirt sleeve
circling it, his fingers in thick hair—but sensed it alert,
awake. Awake. —That's what this was. A great wave had
come along and knocked him flat; washed him up,
tossed him up—belly-up on the beach.

The rattling was snow; icing; beads striking glass.

"Now you be careful, Mister Warshaw. You be serious. You hear me?" The small cautious face pushed and
peeped at the crack in the door. The old woman had
been whispering—because it was dark—and that made
the candle spurt. Two wicks flickered in the concentric
circles of her glasses. Her trembling head reminded
Leo of an infant's head; insulted, indignant, wobbling
on a weak neck.

"Mind you don't blow it out!" she scolded.

"You be careful yourself, Missus C. And I'll be serious, I promise. If you like, I'll hold my breath all the way
down."

The bolt clacked in the lock, the chain scraped. It was
a short way across the hall to the service stairs, a spiral
of iron rail and concrete steps. Going down was harder
for Leo, dragging his leg after, so much dead weight.

He counted to himself, getting his bearings. —Twelve steps, a sort of landing. A turn. Four steps more, a wider landing. Another turn. —He went sideways, the candle in one hand, sliding his glove along the wall. An ochre color, yellow mush. The stuccoed paint shone: bumps and blisters.

He stepped on something.

Leo was pretty sure now he had let out a yell. He hoped it wasn't as loud as he thought. The light shook as he held it up.

What he saw was a sack. Old clothes. A man. Lying on his face, his head in his arm, shoulders rising and falling in his tight jacket. A seam split under one sleeve. Next to his elbow a pair of spectacles stuck in black glue. Blood.

"Buddy? Hey, buddy?"

Leo nudged him with a toe.

A waft of cold air, the dankness of sewer pipes. The man's breath was releasing a familiar smell.

So. A wino. But he must have had a pretty bad fall, poor bugger. The change had rolled out of his pockets; pennies, nickels, scattered on the landing. One shoe off and one shoe on. A dirty sock, a bare heel—was that what Leo had stepped on? His hair was thin, scalp wearing through; the back of his neck mottled and shiny. So were his knuckles; a swollen scaly sheen.

Ringworm?

Now what made him think of that. A childhood disease. He hadn't so much as heard the word in forty years. And he had never been too sure just what it was in the first place; only that it was catching. Well, this looked catching, if anything did: the sloughing skin, the scanty hair, the two dark purplish ears.

The candle hissed and smoked, a thin black thread.

In the street it would have been easy to do the decent thing, go for help, find a phone, hail a passing squad car. But what to do here? Shout through the halls? Knock on doors? Who would answer? Who would care? Was there any reason why they should? —He saw how they lived here, hiding behind their locks and chains, afraid of each other and the dark. A drunk on the stairs. Nothing to get excited about. Could be a nightly occurrence. Maybe this same guy; maybe he made a regular habit of it. Maybe he was used to sleeping it off on the stairs.

"Buddy? Hey? Buddy?"

Leo bent down, laid a glove on the man's shoulder. A grunt and the head rolled on the crook of the arm. A slab of unshaved cheek, an edge of loose wet lip. Pretty tanked up, all right, and he'd have to be—out on a night like this. No coat, his jacket and pants worn thin as old dollars. And only one shoe. What about the other?

The dirt-crusted sock; the bare gristly heel. Callused, yellowed—a chicken spur.

For the first time it crossed Leo's mind. What if this guy hadn't fallen down drunk? What if he'd been mugged? The greasy glasses. The blood. The scattered pennies. Someone could have grabbed his coat, gone through his pockets. But what did the lousy sneak thief have to hit him for? Drunk as this guy was, would he have put up a fight?

And wait—he was being slow tonight. He'd just been this way with the old lady, right? And that was, what? Five, ten minutes ago? —He had shined the flashlight in her closet, her bathtub, under her bed; helped her

get the gas oven going to warm up a bit; she had fished
this stump of utility candle out of a drawer. —Say ten.
Ten minutes; it couldn't have been more. No laundry
sack, no dirty socks, no loose coins then. Nothing on the
stairs. If it had happened at all, it had happened just
now. And the mugger—if there was a mugger—might
still be there. Might be watching this very minute.

Leo sensed the other, half crouched, as Leo was,
holding his breath.

"Buddy! Hey!"

Louder, leaning closer, shaking the shoulder. Leo
held out the candle, as if to examine the man by the
fitful light. He was examining his options. What did he
have on him? A wallet. That was nothing; he never
carried more than a few bucks at a time. A watch. Ouch,
that hurt. A new one and a damn good one too. His
coat. The plot thickens. Good for you, he thought; talking to the mugger—already on familiar terms. Not a bad
haul. Bet you never expected to make a score in this
dump, did you? This must be your lucky night.

Well, why not? How about it? What was to stop him
from talking to the mugger? Actually. Out loud. Making
a deal. How would it go? —Come on, be reasonable.
You never had it so easy. Who needs any rough stuff?
Why exert yourself? Why go to the trouble? All you
have to do is ask. Honest. Believe me.

Take what you want and no hard feelings.

Talking out loud. That was a hot one. To whom? To
what? Wasting his breath. How did he know there was
anyone there? And if there was? So what?—*Be reasonable.* Look who he was asking to *be reasonable.* Who ever
said a mugger had to *be reasonable.* This one probably
liked his work, loved it, got a big kick out of it. Busting

glasses, cracking heads. That's what he was in business for. Just for the fun of it.

Anyone who would swipe the coat off a scabby old wino.

Not to let on. That was the main thing. That would expose him—invite an attack. He remembered someone, it must have been his father, giving him that advice:

The dog will bite you if it knows you're scared.

His father, for sure. Just like the old man, just the sort of thing he would say. Dog-eat-dog; some philosophy. Leo still felt the injustice of it. What kind of world was this, anyhow? What could you expect from life, if those were the rules? *The dog will bite you if it knows you're scared.*

He saw himself as a small quivering child; and inside the small quivering child was another—still smaller, still quivering. And so on and so on. And even if you could stop it, keep it from showing on the outside—you couldn't stop being scared, could you? You couldn't help what was inside you? It must be true; it was too bad not to be true; his marrow was mud.

And the dog will know it.

But what was he thinking of? Dogs! Dogs smell fear, have an instinct for it. Dogs attack with animal logic, an animal sixth sense. Why was he worrying about dogs? Then it struck him. The mugger was an animal. Humans are animals. He, Leo—an animal too. A large, lame one. His leg, dammit. He couldn't outrun a turkey. What a target he must make, with his big bald forehead (how lurid its glow by candlelight) and that blunt fleshy space right between his eyes. The brow of an ox, an elephant, a buffalo.

Somewhere in the dark the mugger was waiting, with

his mugger's weapon—whatever that was—and his mugger's advantage. Surprise.

"Buddy? Buddy?"

Leo shook the shoulder again; a gesture of farewell, almost of fellowship. The man groaned into his sleeve; slipping away from him; sinking further into drunkenness, unconsciousness, or sleep. As Leo rose, hanging on to the wall, and before he could let himself think twice about it—he blew out the candle.

"Leo? Leo? What is it? What's the matter?"

Sydney never slept when he dozed off like this; she lay awake, under the weight of his arm, her cheek to his chest, trying not to disturb him. Like a child, hating to get smothered and squeezed, but needing affection too much to refuse it in any form. She could tell he was awake; his breathing had changed; no longer putt-putting away under his mustache. This was less noisy and more wary.

Ever since he had come back tonight, she had sensed something wrong, and she was sure she knew what. Always the same thing. She knew very well that she played a minor role in his life—just as he played a major role in hers; and yet, whenever anything went wrong, or she thought it had; at his slightest frown or change in mood; whatever happened between them—she was ready to take the blame. She would rack her brains, trying to think what it was, what she had done or failed to do; what could have been different. If, she would think. If this and if that. If only.

If. If. If.

She had felt guilty about spending a precious Sunday afternoon away from Mark. Why couldn't they have taken him to the park, the zoo? She pictured Mark walking between them, holding each by the hand, flinging hard varnished kernels of Cracker Jacks at the bears. She would have had a chance, then, to show Mark off —show him at his best—share with him the bounty, the refuge of a man.

When she waited for Leo in his office, she would pretend not to hear him coming. Though how could she not? The corridors were bare, the boards creaked with his peg-leg step, dragging weight. His office was on the top floor of the oldest building on campus, being stripped for renovation. It was a gloomy place; the view from the one window forever gray—stone spires, gargoyles, "Sandcastle Gothic"; unseen pigeons percolating on the drainpipes; the electric space heater humming. When the coils turned red they seemed to cringe. There were books, of course; books everywhere; by the foot, the pound; piled on the floor, dumped from cartons, stuffed into steel cabinets that stretched toward the ceiling. As soon as she heard Leo's step, Sydney would take down a book and stare at it in her lap; or dial the phone; or look for pen and paper; just to appear busy, occupied, absorbed; just to let him know that she had many claims on her attention and a great deal on her mind and a lot of things to do—all sorts of things —better things than to sit here and wait for him.

Wasn't she somebody? Didn't she have a life?

And who was she kidding? It was so far from the truth. Her life seemed empty to her; echoing, like these windows and corridors. Some part of her was always waiting for Leo Warshaw; for his lectures, his classes, his phone calls; for his next word or gesture; for his power to lift up her life or cast it down.

If. If. If.

And at the same time and all the time she knew it didn't matter. She couldn't change anything. Nothing she did made any difference and nothing was going to be any different. It would all come out the same; end the same way.

Now it was coming. Now he would say it. She could tell from the very sound of his breathing. The blows of his heart against his chest, in her ear, seemed a preamble.

"Leo? What is it? Tell me? Please?"

His arm tightened its grip; his fingers moved in her hair.

He would have liked to tell her; had meant to, at first, when he came in tonight. He could have made a story out of it, it might be worth a laugh. It was a joke, after all, and the joke was on him.

It hadn't seemed like much, a tiny twitching flame. Now he saw that it was a lot; all that stood between him and the dark. Dark? That wasn't the word for it; they needed another. Solid dark, total dark, dark to all his senses. He was guiding himself down the stairs, both hands against the wall—outstretched—embracing darkness; darkness and nothing else. He could smell it and touch it. He knew his eyes were open, he could feel its pressure on them. A cold steady pressure in the center of his forehead, like the flat of a knife blade. His mother used to do that, when he got a bump. She chilled a table knife on the block of ice in the wooden chest, and held it to his forehead and pressed. Her face—the oval eyes close together, gathering at the roots of her frown—pressed too. His breath came hot and cold.

Fear? Sure, it was fear. But not that terrible, after all. Because it was here—now—nothing behind, nothing ahead. So this was it, the elusive present. Was that all there was to it? Step by step? He had never been so much in it, of it, in his life.

"Leo?"

She was such a pretty thing, she was so anxious to please. He was grateful to her for being so anxious and so pretty; and if they had made love, he would be grateful for that too. How childlike her beauty was; that was its perfection. He hadn't realized, until he saw the child face to face—a reflection of her face. The lashes so bashful, the cheeks so bold; and all of it no more than a setting for the eyes. Their gaze was so direct, in the midst of all that foliage, it made you feel you must be eavesdropping. True, when Sydney looked most intent, it might mean she was flattering him, trying to seem attentive; not really listening to a word he said. When she was actually paying attention—it happened, now and then—her gaze wandered, her face crumpled, worried and distracted; the way people look when they think they might sneeze.

—That was all he was interested in, she thought; her face. Only because she was young and pretty. Only. Was that all? Was it such a small thing, then? Youth and beauty? To her, maybe. But not to him.

Her cheek felt warm against his chest, her ear laid over his heart—listening, like a physician. Waiting for him to say something, to speak some word; wisdom, enlightenment, a secret or praise. He thought of her defenseless sighs in the dark. Had he really let out a yell? Why should it seem so humiliating? There was nobody there. There never was. The drunk. The raw meat of his neck. The earthworm lip.

He often had insomnia; woke suddenly, coming to his

senses, taken by surprise; wondering where he was, what he was doing wherever he was. But it had been a while since he had waked like this. There was no way of knowing, of course. No one can say for sure. But when you wake—like this—as from a blow, in ambush, caught in a trap—on the whole you think No. No, it's not likely. No and again No. Nothing there. Nothing next. Nothing more.

Some joke. A mugger on the stairs.

But he wasn't ready to make light of it. Not just yet, not right now. Something told him that would be a transgression, a kind of sacrilege. As feelings go, this was pure, it was absolute. Mugger or no mugger—the fear was real.

The snow rattled the window, glass on glass.

"It's okay. It's nothing." He spoke in a whisper, into her hair, stroking it with thick fingers. An ineffectual sort of tenderness. "Something that happened, that's all. I was just thinking about it. I'll tell you another time."

Her cheek rubbed buttons, grizzled hairs. It was all right, a promise. Another time. Another chance. If.

"There's just one thing I'd like to know. If you don't mind a personal question. What've you got that window wide open for, on a night like this? You trying to freeze a guy to death? Aren't you cold too?"

THE
LIFE
YOU
GAVE
ME

So my father is going to be all right.

That's what my mother said as soon as we met at the airport. That's what the doctor said when he came out of surgery. That's what my father said himself, just before he went in, making it snappy over long-distance: "This is costing you money."

That's what I thought all along.

He's always been all right before.

Before. That would be ten years by now.

The voice over the telephone sounded encouraging.

"Mrs. Horner? Sally Horner?"

Uh-huh, he's selling something, was my first thought. What'll it be? Magazine subscriptions? Rug shampooing?—I can never make up my mind what to do about telephone solicitors. Is it better to say No, thanks, and hang up on the spot, so they don't waste any breath? Or to stand there, frowning, with the phone to your ear, and let them finish?

I stood there.

"This is Reverend Nightswan? Chaplain at Covenant Community Hospital?"

Still inquiring.

Didn't I tell you? Collecting for charity. But what's he calling me for? What does he want from me? How did he ever get hold of my name?

"I'm calling about your father? He had an accident?"

"How?"

Owww.

A grappling hook got tangled in seaweed.

"Now take it easy now. Don't go getting all excited. There's nothing to upset yourself about. He fell? Off a ladder? Fixing the roof on the house? It looks like he maybe cracked a couple of ribs, he broke his nose. Things like that. We should know pretty soon. They're still checking him over."

Oh yes. Wasn't that just like him? Easy to picture my father up on a ladder. Haven't I seen him dozens of times? The wide back and heavy shoulders. The polar bear neck. The legs powerful, foreshortened, condensed by their own strength and weight. That's nothing new.

But wait a minute. What's going on here? I don't get it. My parents don't have a house anymore. What roof? What house? What business does the old man have—climbing ladders?

Reverend Nightswan spoke.

"We thought you might want to come down?"

"Now?"

I was still frowning. My father does that. Talks into the telephone as if he's getting a bad connection or bad news. His thick forehead bunched; the phone squeezed to his raspy cheek; raising his voice to make himself heard in the next room—the next world. He says he can't help it, he's used to working in the plant, shouting over machines. I believe him. I got sent every now and

then to pick up his paycheck. Through all the open
transom windows the noise made a tunnel: clubbing,
bludgeoning, plundering air.

He doesn't know his own strength, says my mother.

We have the same vertical groove over one eyebrow;
more than a frown—almost a scar.

"You mean right now?"

"Well, yes. Now. Now would be good. Now, that is,
if it's all right with you."

"Yeah, sure," I said. "Okay. Now."

It was a warm bright day. Earlier a pair of window
washers had been at work, ropes and planks butting the
cemented slabs of the building. I heard voices, looked
out, down they came. Thick boots, army pants, cigarettes in curly beards. The sponges slopped and
slurred. Water blurted. It ran on the glass as over stones
glazed in a stream.

The sky looked like that. Transparent. Luminous.

Out of the clear blue sky it came to me: What if my
father was dead?

That must be it. That was what they had called me
for. That was what it was all about. The Chaplain. No
wonder. You know yourself how they are; they never
tell you the truth. They don't like to break the news over
the phone.

I pictured a form under a white sheet; my father laid
out like a large piece of furniture. The hulk of the chest,
the humps and ridges of the toes, the sloping head, the
bump of the nose.

Didn't that guy just say, though, that my father's nose
was broken? He wouldn't say that, would he, if my fa-

ther was dead? No, no one would say a thing like that. Not a broken nose.

He must be all right, then.

He was going to be all right.

I felt grateful to this Reverend Nightswan, whoever he was. My first guess had come pretty close. —A limited-one-time-only offer. Can't-last. Take-it-or-leave-it.

Now or never.

There was something I wanted to say to my father. I knew what it was, what it had to be. Everyone knows that. Only I wasn't sure how to say it. But I always knew the time would come. Sooner or later. The stage would be set; the scene would be played; all of a sudden it would be easy.

All of a sudden I would mean it.

Still, I dreaded seeing him like this. My father's size and strength were more than physical. Mental, temperamental. Character traits. Mind Over Matter was his motto. Whenever anyone else got sick, he would tiptoe about the house, trying to speak softly—lowering his loud voice to sandpaper whispers—pulling down window shades, fetching glasses of water. He looked apologetic, respectful, almost—if such a word could be applied to him—scared; as if he had filled the glass too full and thought it might spill. He gave advice, pep talks, about keeping your head warm and your feet cool. And he meant it. Did he have a Hot Head? Cold Feet? But it was no good. What was the use? Others didn't have the benefit of his constitution—or, as he called it, his System—or his conscience; his maxims or his morals. To see him brought down, laid low, damaged, hurting, like any other injured creature—was to see him disgraced.

All of which is not to say that my father was ever a simple man. Only that he didn't know his own strength.

But I did.

The Emergency Room was busy. The benches facing front, lined up like church pews; peaked caps moving up and down—nurses scribbling away behind a high counter. I spotted my mother standing and talking to a doctor. A large dark man in a Hawaiian sports shirt and tinted glasses; but I could tell he was a doctor from the beeper in his pocket and all the ball-point pens clipped to it. My mother's head came just about up to this row of pens on his chest; thrust at him—close—as if she wanted to take a bite out of him.

It surprises me how short my mother really is.

"He'll be all right, won't he?" she was saying. The doctor folded his arms, braced in steely watchband.

She turned on me.

"Well he's gone and done it now. Now he's really gone and done it. He fixed himself up but good this time," she said. "And I told him too. I told him no more ladders. He's not the man he was, you know. I begged him. Please. Don't go climbing any ladders."

"That's what I don't understand. I can't figure it out. What in the world was he doing on a roof?"

"What was he doing? What do you think he was doing?"

She skimped up the arcs of two picked plucked little

eyebrows—the only items little in that proud front, her face. Hair white; features dark; lipstick intense, vivid as a caste mark.

"Do you have to ask? Don't you know your father by now? A favor, that's what. For the neighbors, that's who. You don't suppose he'd be fixing anything for me? Not him. Not if the ceiling was falling on our heads. He's *retired.* I can't get him to look up from the newspaper. I have to plead with him till I'm blue in the face. But the neighbors are never afraid to ask. All they have to do is knock on the door. —It'll only take you a minute. It's nothing for you. —Oh no. Nothing. Some nothing. Go. Go take a look at him. Go see what's nothing. I just hope he learned his lesson. Maybe next time he'll listen to me for a change. That man. Talking to him is like talking to a wall."

I followed the doctor down the corridor.

We were at a basement level; painted pipes in the ceiling, loud bare floors. His back was humped and husky in his flowery shirt, his arm swinging and flashing its watchband. I tried to picture a hospital room, a row of white beds, and in one of them my father. Looking out from a visor of bandages, a splinted nose.

My father spent his working years in a factory; he was a junk collector, a handyman—fixing and forcing. It wasn't as if he didn't get "banged up," "busted," and "clipped"; chunks taken out of himself on things jagged or rusty; his hairy-backed hands daubed Technicolor from stinging stains and dyes. Orange Mercurochrome, purple permanganate, smelly yellow-brown iodine. His nails were bruised and black as clamshells—more decoration.

His eye would squint, his lip grip. Pain, effort, concentration: all one to him.

But then, remembering his audience—my sister and/or me—and strictly for our benefit, he would give his thick curly head a shake—a shaggy shudder—a wet dog wagging; and pantomime a howl. A yowl. His mouth with its lead-weighted molars opening wide, wrapping all around the sound:

Yow-wooch!

Only nothing came out.

"Sunnuvugun," he'd say. "That was a beaut."

But where were we going? Why was it taking so long? Frosted-glass doors, elevator doors, sliding doors. Doors with portholed windows. The doctor's arm kept swinging. Our heels clicked. Everyone knows the sound of heels clicking in hospital corridors. Everyone knows the tread of the heart.

"In there."

He pushed a door. A long sheeted table stood wheeled under a lamp. The purplish light sputtered. A nurse had been giving the patient a shot, and as she stepped aside, still fussing with the sheets, I caught a glimpse—just a glimpse—of something dark. Black as fur. A forbidden sight: the naked hairy loins of my father.

She tossed some bloody cotton in a bucket.

He had not been cleaned up, prettied up, bound up, and bandaged. His nose was swollen and clotting; his cheeks too—puffed up, punchy—like a boxer's. His whole face was bigger than usual, a damp glistening gray, the color of steamed meat. And the sheets weren't tidy either. They wrinkled and twisted.

I must have come closer. He opened his eyes.

"Oh, Sal."

He looked surprised. Most of the time my father looks surprised; it's because his eyes are so blue. They stand out above the rough cheeks. They startle you too.

Say, what're eyes like you doing in a face like this?

"'Lo, Sal."

At the last minute, feeling that the ladder was slipping and giving way beneath him, he had had the presence of mind, the force, to hurl himself forward. So he had landed, not on the concrete, on the back of his head (and from the height of two stories plus I guess that would have been that)—but on the soft earth, on his face.

He had been wearing his new glasses; so new, no one had had a chance to get used to them yet. The wire rims. The eyes expanded, blinking. They were safety glass and didn't smash, but the impact left their impression on his face—an exact copy.

There they were: two circles in his cheeks, a deep dent over the bridge of his nose.

The eyes opened; they shut.

The eyes opened; they shut.

He seemed to be staring at me through a pair of specs.

He looked very large, he looked formidable; winding sheets, swollen face, broken chest. It was moving, but not up and down—

Higher.

Then higher.

And a little higher.

A boulder being pushed uphill.

He seemed to be concentrating on the effort.

His lids were violet, an odd cosmetic effect. His lip gripped—stiffened—things better left unsaid.

This wasn't what I was expecting. Not what I feared, but not what I hoped. Clearly, this was more than a case of a couple of cracked ribs and a broken nose. This wasn't going to be so easy. No one was going to get off that lightly. The sheets were wrapped and wrung about him. They clung to him. They were the pain.

He nodded, eyes shut, chin to his chest.

"'S all right, Sal."

What did he mean, it's all right?

That he was going to be all right?

That things were all right between us? (Just like that?)

Or only that it was all right, I had done my duty, shown my face; now I could go?

One thing for sure. I was dismissed. This wasn't the time, and there was nothing to say. It was an old story. I had come to ask, to seek, to plead—and not to give.

I backed out, shut the door.

"Gone . . . done it . . ." I heard him mutter.

The doctor was passing; I caught up with him.

"He'll be all right, won't he?"

He folded his arms. It was hard to hold his eyes, in the tinted glasses.

"We have to wait and see."

"But he'll be all right? He's going to be all right?"

He didn't seem to know what I was asking.

Well? What are we waiting for?

We know what's coming, don't we? We know what direction it's coming from? Is it a secret? A rumor? We know what has to happen sometime. Why keep putting it off?

Now? You mean right now?

The woman sitting next to me on the plane was on her way to see her folks in Florida too.

"I'm dreading this," she told me.

Her parents were in their eighties, had been living in Florida the past ten or a dozen years. Up to a few months ago their health had been holding up pretty well; then both had broken down at once. Between them they had just about everything wrong: cancer, heart, kidneys, cataracts, diabetes. "You name it." There was no hope, of course; no question of recovery. The only question was *how long.* She hadn't made up her mind, didn't know what to do; didn't know what she would find when we finally got on the ground. She wasn't sorry the plane had been delayed.

"Though I guess I have to face it sometime."

There had been a freak spring storm, clear across the country—taking more or less the route we were covering now—dumping ice and sleet, cracking trees, downing power lines. The world was a snow swamp; the Everglades turned white. Knee-deep drifts, rafting logs, broken branches; limbs bent low under loads of snow like lush tropical vegetation. Everything bowed down in silence.

Now we were flying over yet another snowy landscape; three-dimensional cutout clouds. The plane was packed; stewardesses in ascots and aprons pushing carts, passing out drinks, paper napkins, sliding stacked snack trays over our seats. Their faces leaned and smiled, sunny with makeup. Ice cubes faintly tinkled in plastic glasses. Smokers in the rear section had lighted up, cigarette fumes seeping through the compartment; stale traces, a bluish tinge, leaking like the trail of a dye marker.

The aisle was lit with wintry brightness.

"It's awfully bad luck," she said. "It's really a very bad break."

Somehow she had been expecting to deal with these matters one at a time.

She was in her fifties (I'd say); round face, pouchy chin, small neat-tipped mobile nose. Bifocals. Frizzy gray hairs straggling from a smooth dark bun. (By no means as much tinsel as I have; premature gray runs in my mother's family. We like to call it premature.)

She picked up her sandwich in plump ringed fingers and eyed it suspiciously. "Wonder what's in this? Ugh. Don't you hate airplane food?"

She put it back on her plate and began to dissect it with her fork.

I told her that my parents had only recently moved to Florida, after talking about it for years.

"Mine were that way too," she said. "Kept putting it off."

Now they loved it; they were only sorry they hadn't made the move much sooner.

"Just like mine," she said. "Same with mine. Don't I know."

Luckily they were barely seventy; still in good health; still plenty able to enjoy themselves.

"Oh, mine were too," she said. "Mine were too."

She was glancing at the window, not really looking out, the light settled—a kind of sediment—in the thick bottoms of her lenses. She didn't need to look; she knew the terrain. She had been here before, she had covered this ground. She was drawing me a map.

Each time she spoke, she nodded and swallowed—as if given permission—and poked at her lips with the paper napkin.

"Mine too. Mine too."

I didn't say that my father had undergone surgery that morning.

It was an emergency. A couple of nights before, he had started to hemorrhage. He was in bed; he got up and put his pants on and drove himself and my mother to the hospital. She drives now; but not with him in the car. By the time they got there, some twenty minutes later, the pants, the front seat, and the assortment of rags he keeps in the car for old times' sake (there's not much place for his junk in their new apartment, their new lives) were soaked through; sticky-bright; red with burst blood. He had almost no pulse. He had been on intravenous feedings and transfusions. The doctors were expecting to remove a section of the colon; they were pretty sure it would be malignant. But if all went well and there were no complications, they were pretty sure he would be cured completely.

Who knows why they kept putting it off?

My father had been retired for years, had elected to take an early retirement, first chance he got. It was something new. Now there are bonuses; then there were penalties. It meant a considerable sacrifice of pensions and benefits. But he didn't want to be one of those, as he put it—as he was bound to—Living on Borrowed Time. Besides, he had always hated his job. Not that he said so. Not that he had to.

I used to wake to the trudge of a shovel: my father scraping the coal pile, getting the fire going in the furnace, in the basement. Hollow pipes carried it all through the house. The hoarse flinty rumbling had something of the ring and register—the grumbling resonance—of his voice, and I would think of him as down there talking to himself.

Down in the dumps.

That was not just a figure of speech, with my father.

Outside it would still be dark. The snow on roofs, gutters, fences, clotheslines, nothing but gloom. The air was black-and-blue with cold.

That was when we lived on the West Side of Chicago, a neighborhood of two-story houses, mostly frame. In winter the sidewalks were blasted black from the dust of coal delivery trucks, clinkers and ashes sprinkled on snow and ice; in summer, from the squashed juices of the mulberry trees. Our windows faced west, smeared with angry red sunsets. I remember the day we moved in. I mean the day my father moved us in; hauling it all down three flights from our old flat, tying it on top of his car, hauling it back up the skinny front steps, the porch on stilts. Everybody else watched, neighbors old and new. Crushing his burdens to himself—hugging, squeezing in his hairy arms—with his crouching legs and grim gripping face, he might have been in a wrestling match. A contest of wills.

Now please. Don't get me wrong. My father was never a show-off, a muscle-bound type, like these body builders and pumpers of iron in the slick magazines; arms and chests molded in epoxy. You didn't notice his muscles. —Width. Heft. Pelted neck. Hairy withers. Ruddy flesh—almost raw. Smell of head sweat. (It was running from the roots of his curly hair in shining creeks.) And always, always that impression he gave, and still gives, of being laden with strength. Loaded down with it.

When everything was piled up in what was going to be our new front room—all our misplaced, mismated store; boxes, bedsprings, bureau drawers, chairs upside down on the table; all looking pretty dismal and discouraging, dashed with light from bare dirty windows— my father took my sister on one knee and me on the other. He made a speech:

From Now On. Got to Get Organized. Turn Over a New Leaf. All Pitch In. Do Our Part. Listen to Your Mother. Treat Each Other Right. Make a Fresh Start.

The dresser with the tilted mirror found its way upstairs to the bedroom; the wooden ice chest wound up in the kitchen; everything else stayed where it was. If not those selfsame boxes and drawers, headless lamps, black-bagged vacuum cleaners (why three *Hoover* uprights and no rugs? not that any of them worked)—then others. There was always more where that came from. Still, my mother talked about "redoing"—as if anything had ever been done. That was what everybody else said, and she wanted to be like everybody else. From my friends' houses I knew the sort of thing she had in mind.

Carpets you couldn't walk on, sofas you couldn't sit on, drapes you couldn't draw (the sun might fade the carpets and upholstery). Something too good for us to use. —When she got her carpets, she said, "the Traffic" would take their shoes off at the door. When she got her towels, "the Traffic" would dry their hands on paper. When she got her bedspreads, "the Traffic" would hang up their clothes.

"The Traffic": that was us.

She was giving aid and comfort to the enemy.

We must have lived in that house a dozen years (which surprises me; I thought it was a hundred), and all that time it looked as if we had just moved—or were just about to. How could she ever "have anything"?

After they sold the house and my father retired, they moved a lot; Lock, Stock & Barrel; which was about all they had to their name. They were like fugitives keeping a jump ahead of the law. So when they decided, after years of this, to move to Florida, everyone pooh-poohed:

A Retirement Village? Now I've heard everything. Are they out of their minds? All those *old people?* Phooey. And what will they do with themselves? Sit around and play cards? And the houses—all alike. You can't tell them apart. (A good thing they don't drink; they'd never find their way home.) Living in a fishbowl. No privacy. Everybody knowing everybody's business. Don't worry. They'll get tired of it. They'll be back. Just like all the other times.

When it comes to decisions, my parents like to change their minds a few times; otherwise they don't feel right about it; same way a dog likes to turn around and around before it lies down. But they put a couple of boxes in somebody's basement, and a couple more in somebody's attic, and piled the pots and pans and the portable TV into the back of the car and drove down. To Live Happily Ever After. From Now On.

All at once the clouds ended. Came skidding to a halt at an edge of blue sky, as banks of snow and ice stop at the blue edge of the sea. I saw a curved shore, a stiff-frozen surf. I knew it was an illusion, but the illusion was complete. The plane was moving through light as a boat through water. The air was vibrating with clarity and brightness; the nose cones of the jets were tingling with it—ringing out—as if they had been struck with tuning forks.

The engines roar.

The light is loud and clear.

"Bad luck," she kept saying. "A very bad break."

Sometimes I wonder what we look like, to stewardesses. Passengers, strapped into our seats, our trays down in front of us. Infants in high chairs, maybe? Clamoring to be fed? Here we were, side by side, the two dutiful daughters—she with her prompt obedient manners, close-mouthed possessive nibbles that made me think of a squirrel in the grass; me with my napkin tucked under my chin (where it belongs).

So here I am at last. This is it; this is what it's like; I finally made it. Not just what I expected, though. Hard to say just what that was. Maybe I thought the scenery would be better. Panoramic. Valleys, vistas, mountain peaks. Pearly clouds, purple distances. The sun sending down planks of light. Yes. That's right. A *view.* This is pretty flat, you know. —Will I be her in ten years' time?

Then what? What when I am in her shoes? She doesn't know what to do because she doesn't want to do it. Easy for me to say. But what will I do?

"I know it sounds awful," she said. "It's a terrible thing to say. And yet. Right now. If one of them, at least. Isn't it crazy? You always think it's the worst thing that can happen. And then all of a sudden it seems like the best thing."

Maybe it's just the only thing.

"But my parents are very, very happy," I said.

She nodded and swallowed and patted her lips:

"Give them ten years."

And now for the hard part. My father and I were not on the best of terms, not on the worst. No finalities, no formal estrangements. Words had been spoken—plenty of words; but not the most bitter. Not the Last Word. Nothing that couldn't be taken back.

We hadn't shot all the arrows in our quivers.

In his heart of hearts (I truly believe) my father held this against himself. Does a man have to live in this way? Should a man put up with such things? Disappointment, disaffection, disobedience? Unnaturalness between parents and children? Strictly observant Orthodox Jews have ways of dealing with offenders; settling matters for once and for all. They know how to cut their losses. An offspring who has transgressed, sinned against the tribe and tradition, can be read off—cast out—given up for dead.

The Prayers are recited; the Period of Mourning is observed; the Tears are shed.

Goodbye and good riddance.

My father admired these methods, and had long been threatening to use them. He had been threatening as long as I could remember. How Sharper Than a Serpent's Tooth It Is to Have a Thankless Child. That was one of his favorite sayings. (I could tell from his lofty look he wasn't making it up.) If I heard it once, I heard it a thousand times, and never without a thrill—a shiver —of guilt and shame: a sense of my destiny. This was prophecy!

Wasn't it his right? Wasn't it his duty? Give him one good reason why he shouldn't.

Was he a Jew for nothing?

There was only one hitch. My father is not a strictly observant Orthodox Jew. He does as others do. Sometimes he Observes. Sometimes he Looks the Other Way.

He observes—when he observes—in the Orthodox manner. He walks to the synagogue in skullcap and prayer shawl and stands up and prays with the book in his hands. The smooth circle on his head, the sprinkled drops of his Brilliantine, make him look stiff and anointed. His hoarse gristly throat locked in necktie and collar, his eyes blue and blinking above grouty cheeks. The room sways; fringes quiver; my father's rough raspy voice gets rougher and louder. When he turns the page, or loses his place, it drops to a mutter; his chin drops to his chest.

His lip is full, solemn—exposed.

Even these days, down in Florida, he insists on walking to the synagogue: two or three miles of heat, open highway, diesel trucks, potholes, exploding rubber; mag-wheeled pickups sporting the spokes of the Confederate flag on their bumpers, and horns that hoot 'n' toot and whistle "Dixie." He persists: there is no Orthodox synagogue to walk to. And my mother comes stumbling after, in billowy skirts and high heels, scared to death he will get knocked down and run over if she's not there to keep an eye on him. —What a target. His broad, brunt-bearing shoulders draped in stripes, silk and fringes; his curly hair whitened, thickened; the glasses pressing his cheeks. Every few minutes she stops to lean on him for support, to rattle the stones out of her shoes, to ask an old question:

Why can't he take the car and drive?

Why can't he be like everybody else?

But this went on only a few days out of the year; on Rosh Hashanah, Yom Kippur, and those occasions (ever increasing) when my father recited prayers for the dead. Of other holidays, my sister and I scarcely heard the names. We fasted on Yom Kippur, kept Passover faithfully, didn't mix meat and milk at the table or eat of "any abominable thing." But we didn't keep kosher. No separate sets of dishes, no meat ritually slaughtered, no chickens hanging by their feet—in dishonor—in the kosher butcher's window with twisted necks and pincered wings. My parents lighted candles in memory of the dead; pink-labelled glasses filled with a white wax that sizzled. Afterwards we used them for drinking glasses; they matched and made a set. (Just about the only thing that ever did.) But in our house prayers and blessings were not said. I never saw my mother light candles on Friday night. Her own mother did. The old lady would mutter the prayer hastily to herself, under her breath, holding both hands up to her face: as if, I thought, the flames might be too bright for her. They never seemed that bright to me. Still I saw their reflection—refraction—in her eyes.

Once, on a trip, we visited the family of my uncle's bride; Pennsylvania Dutch Quakers living in the Lebanon Valley. They were plain, but not like the Amish farmers we had seen along the way, with their clip-clopping horses and dipping buggy whips. Mr. K. wore buttons on his pants, drove a car, used farm machinery. He was a tall wide old man and his hair had the solid whiteness of a salt lick. And his wife, for all her starched cap and apron, did not look as reticent as the Amish wives—sheltered under their bonnets and wagon canopies, the horses waiting, horse-patient, with black flies on their eyelids and black blinders. Her cheeks were broad and bright as crockery. (They really did remind me of all those cups and bowls, glazed and blazoned with slogans, selling at every roadside stand. "Too Soon Old and Too Late Smart." "The Butter Is All.")

It was August, and it was hot. The cows were mud puddles under the trees. The grass was so blurred with heat it didn't look cool; gassy, rather, effervescent; something like the green lights burping up the sides of jukeboxes, or a sweet soda pop, in vogue at the time, called *Green River*.

The house seemed lighter inside than out. Criss-crossed windows, white cloth, china cabinets gleaming with cut glass, silver, pewter, that had been in the family two hundred years. Platters heaped with fresh tomatoes, fresh peaches—sliced, juicy, running with their own ripeness—and dark sizzling meat.

We sat down to eat.

The meat had a strange flavor I had not tasted before. As soon as I bit in, I knew something was wrong. I stopped and looked up, mouth full, head over my plate. I wasn't the only one; my mother and my little sister were looking up too. We glanced at each other and we glanced at my father. He wasn't looking at anyone. His fork was lifted and his eyes were lowered. He seemed to crouch over the table, his head so low between his big shoulders I could see the back of his neck—which was as wide as a brick; and his ears—which were as red.

Curtains fidgeted at the windows. An electric fan blew on us as on hot soup. Our host and hostess were fanning us too, flapping at our faces with fly swatters, dish towels, anything that came to hand. Their glasses beamed—almost urgently solicitous. Beads of sweat prospered on their brows.

Through the screen I could see fields wavering vaguely in the heat, and the raised hackles of the hills.

My father laid down his fork and raised up his eyes.

"Very good," he said, reaching for the water glass.

He nodded. He gulped.

"Very good."

His jaws moved on their haunches; his molars collided. At once, as at a signal, we all began to chew. Life was going to continue.

Naturally, we knew better than to bring up this subject when we got back to the car. (Just as we knew not to talk when my father was shifting gears; there was something wrong with the clutch.) And what was there to say? That he had eaten ham—pig—for that is what it was; had permitted his wife and daughters to eat—rather than to give offense? No, there was more to it. For himself, he would not have been so touchy. What

he couldn't bring himself to do was to let on—let these
good kind people know that they were the ones who had
given offense.

God knows, they never intended. Their daughter had
up and married a Jew; she had gone off to live in the big
city; of that much they were aware, but they had a pretty
hazy notion of what it might mean. They were different
too. The world was divided into town folk and country
folk, and those who were plain and those who were not;
and they had trouble enough keeping track of what set
them apart from everybody else—without worrying
about every little quibbling distinction, what the fuss
was about, amongst all the rest.

So far so good. That much a Jew could understand.
But there was something else. I felt it then, and I can
try to say it now. The china cabinets, the crisscrossed
windows; the white farmhouses, bricked chimneys; the
fenced fields; the animals harbored under the trees.
(Through the screen there was the stillness of a canvas
someone had painted on in numbers.) They had all this
to uphold them in their ways, sustain them in their
differences. Our connection seemed more puzzling. We
had nothing but this: the grip of our rituals.

Sometimes it's hard to know the right thing to do.

I'm sure my father held this against himself as well.
And yet he had no use for Conservative, much less
Reform; practices which would at least have let him off
the hook. He was always a man to take his own measure;
but what good are rules, if you make them up as you go
along?

And still, you see what comes of it, living with com-
promise. (As if it is his fault that there are things
we have to live with—and things we have to live with-

out.) Let that be a lesson. If only he had been reli-
gious enough—righteous enough—man enough—mad
enough. But who was he to perform such sonorous rites
over me? Chanting Prayers for the Dead? Weeping and
rocking and tearing his beard?

How would it look?

What would he tear?

He doesn't even have a beard.

So my father remains at a loss to express his dissatis-
faction. He tries: When he wrote his will, he cut me out.
(I know; he showed me; he couldn't wait.) Not What a
Daughter Should Be, read the clause, in a style I think
I recognize by now. That was when at long last it
dawned. —Dummy! I am, and always have been, just
the sort of daughter he wanted. What with one thing
and another, all things considered—the times we live
in, the Spirit of the Age—I am What a Daughter Should
Be. Just What a Daughter Should Be. Just that and no
more.

It's nothing to brag about.

It was raining a little, a fresh-scented driz-
zle; it might have been salt spray blowing from the
ocean. The breeze felt soft as a scarf. I saw it drifting
around my mother as she stood in front of the spot-
lighted palms; floating through the folds of her skirt,
the white filaments of her hair. Trees leaned, turned

inside out like beach umbrellas. People were rushing to make their planes, lugging armloads of grapefruit. Grapefruit, grapefruit everywhere. In string bags, in plastic, packed in crates on crinkly green cellophane. Bald, thick-skinned grapefruit; yellow, uniform; perfect spheres. That was how to tell who was coming from who was going. The ones trying to take home replicas of the sun.

My mother looks like someone in disguise.

She is stained teak color from the Florida sun, so tan her lipstick seems to be glowing in the dark. (Purple-pink; bougainvillea.) Her hair is cut short, shingled, clinging to her cheeks—her face enclosed in white petals—like the fancy rubber bathing caps ladies wear down here. Her shoulders stoop. (Since when?) Her elbows stick out. (How long has this been going on?) Her legs, big knee-knobs, are two thick black bones.

I recognized her anyhow. I always have, so far.

It was late—too late to go to the hospital tonight—the air so thick, spongy, saturated, I felt I could stop right then and there and peel it off me in layers, same as the northern sweaters I was wearing. But my mother was heading for the car, in a hurry, her high heels striking the sidewalk. She walks fast—especially now; luggage or no luggage, it would be hard to keep up with her. And she wears steel taps on her heels; it emphasizes her pace. Each step rings out—announcing her. That's her signal; you hear her coming. It's a practical matter, though; it saves shoe leather. All foresight, that's my mother. Alas, no hindsight.

She stopped. "I don't want you to say anything about that."

"About what?" I said.

"About that. You know what. What you just said. I don't want you saying anything about it to him."

The biopsy report wasn't back yet.

"But what do you mean? Is there something wrong? Something else? There's nothing to hide?"

"Never mind. I just don't want him worrying, that's all. He doesn't need to know anything about it."

"But, Mother," I said.

"No buts about it. You heard me. You're not to say anything, and that's that. That's all there is to it."

My mother may be short; but she has the manner, the bearing, the imperious white head and noble features (Roman coin? Indian-head nickel?) of a woman who is used to getting what she wants. Having her own way. And she has the reputation, besides. "Won't take no for an answer." And yet—as far as I know—and except in the most trivial circumstances—she never gets what she wants; she never has her own way (whatever that is). No one ever "listens" to her.

She doesn't let that stop her. No harm in trying. And maybe, if she can just keep it up long enough. . . . In the meantime, it's true; she doesn't take no for an answer. She doesn't take answers.

She went tap-tapping on, elbows sharp and crooked and ready at her sides; head thrust forward—sleuthlike, I thought—its whiteness all but phosphorescent under the eerie purple of the arc lamps. In the spotlights, palms dipped their green pennants. Her heels clipped the cement. Her pleated skirts whipped where her hips used to be. The drummer no one is marching to.

She glanced at me over the hill of her back:
"You'll do as I say," she told me.

Once, when my sister and I came downstairs to go to school, our father was still sitting at the table, dragging the spoon through his coffee cup; one arm white with bandages, in a sling. He had cut his wrist on the power saw; the blood came up in black bullets, spluttered the ceiling; he knew he had hit an artery.

He tied the arm in a tourniquet—tightened it in his teeth—and drove to the Emergency Room.

"That was a close call," he said. "Thought I was a goner."

(He did not smoke or drink or use what he called "phraseology." "There'll be no phraseology in this house!" But he had plenty of phrases of his own. Customers, Characters, Fakers, Jokers, Schemers, Dreamers, Screwballs, Bellyachers, Stinkers, Sleepers, So-and-Sos, and Yo-Yos. Just to give a hint; a partial listing. But the greatest of these was Goner.

Goner! Goner! The very word was like a bell.)

And he shook his head and whistled appreciatively and went on stirring.

Later my mother took me aside.

"Daddy was very hurt," she said. "You didn't even say you're sorry. What's the matter with you? Haven't you got a mouth on you? Are you afraid to talk? *I'm sorry you hurt yourself, Daddy.* Is that too much to say?"

My mother, of course, was the family interpreter. She translated—explained—excused us to each other. That was her job, and she had her work cut out for her; but I used to think she made most of it up:

He doesn't mean it.

This hurts him more than it hurts you.

You know he really loves you.

He's *still* your father!

You see what I mean. Who'd fall for that? As if she expected us to swallow such stuff. —And just because she said a thing was so didn't mean it was so. Maybe my father had said something, and maybe he hadn't. Maybe she *thought* he was hurt. Maybe—and this most likely— she thought he *ought* to be hurt. Because it wasn't only that she put words in our mouths; she was trying to "redo" us.

She's so sensitive.

That was her excuse for me. That was how she sought to put an end to their endless quarrels; on and on, like the freight cars bickering in the switchyard. —"Can't you see she's sensitive?" I happened to know I wasn't sensitive; unless it meant throwing up. I didn't even want their quarrels to end! Not in that way. I wanted an end that would be an end; something dramatic—if need be, drastic. I didn't care what or how.

"Don't provoke him." That was another one. Wishful thinking. I guess she liked to think that he could be provoked because that implied an opposite. But my sister and I knew better; our father's wrath was made of sterner stuff. We had simply got in the way of it; we were too small for it; it preceded us. Not that that didn't make us feel smaller.

"You're asking for it. You've got one coming. You're going to get a going-over."

Leaning on his elbows over the newspaper, not bothering to lift his eyes from the page. We could see blue roving from the bottom of one column to the top of the next. When he wasn't shouting at the top of his voice, stretching his throat and straining his vocal cords, his tone was something more felt than heard. Cadenced blows. The freight trains shuddering through the night; the grunts coming up from the basement.

Sure, don't provoke him. Go tell the trees not to provoke the wind. All that quaking makes it nervous.

These scenes are lapped by lurid flames of memory.

I seem to recall them taking place down in the basement, next to the coal pile. Spiders spilling down walls, pipes furred with dust, the dangling light bulb swaying violently on its wire. (His head was always bumping into it.) The furnace swelling and glowing with cast-iron heat; orange as the fire within. And so forth. But I know that can't be. It all took place in the kitchen, only the kitchen; the smell of wiped oilcloth, still wet; dishes slanting in the drainboard; the pink-labelled glasses rinsed and turned down. The light as dull as waxed linoleum.

I was the older one, so I went first. My little sister would cling to my mother's legs, hiding her face in my mother's apron and pleading:

Don't hit her! Don't hit her!

She kept peeping out to look and hiding her face again.

But oh, how it sparkled. What earnestness. What passion. What big beautiful tears slipped and slid down her big beautiful cheeks. I was impressed. She was weeping zircons.

Meanwhile, my father would be counting the strokes of the strap with words; lip gripping, eye squinting, forehead bunched in a frown. A man taking aim, taking measure, playing a hunch:

Let . . . That . . . Be . . . Lesson . . . Next Time
. . . Know Better . . .

At least I hoped he was counting.

The strap snapped against the leg of the table, the
chair. That scared me; I could hear how hard he was
hitting. Which just went to show how hard he was
restraining himself. It was understood he was forever
restraining himself, his a power that must be held in
check:

This hurts him more than it hurts you.

He was a man who didn't know his own strength.

Came time to change places. Now it was my little
sister's turn to bend over; mine to cling to my mother's
legs and plead.

Don't hit her. Don't hit her.

How halfhearted it sounded, even to my ears. I never
put up the defense for her that she put up for me. The
most I could manage was a few snotty sniffles and a
couple of sticky hiccupy secondhand tears.

Sensitive.

Why do I keep saying *little?* My sister was younger,
yes; and she must have been little when she was born;
but all I know is, when I had the mumps, my parents
thought I was her—because my face got so fat—and
switched us in our cribs. She was bigger and stronger
and more precocious. Not only, at five or six, did she
paint her nails magenta—fingers and toes (my mother
hoped it would keep her from biting them—both—
which it didn't)—she shaved her legs. That was her own
idea; by that time we shared a bed, and the stubble on
her knees scratched me to pieces. She was a great
climber of fences and swinger from trees—strangers
had been known to pick her up and spank her because

she scared the wits out of them with her exploits—and, as the tomboy, our father's favorite. He had been disappointed when his firstborn did not turn out to be a boy. That was an open secret. On the other hand, I had a secret of my own. I knew I had spared him a much greater disappointment. Such a boy as I would have been.

Toward books my father's attitude was lofty, as of something he had sworn off, a reformed zealot. He had read a book or two himself, *Oliver Twist* and *The Merchant of Venice*—high school requirements—and he had a theory about the great and famous writers. Therefore, whenever he spotted me, sitting over the hot-air register (the warmest place in the house; the grill left red welts on my legs, checks and boxes just like the ones we used to draw for the game of X-and-O, and I figured people could play on them for the rest of my life)— whenever he spotted me, yet another pile of pages open in my lap—he would hitch up a mighty eyebrow and thicken his forehead:

"Now what? Not another anti-Semite?"

And yet he liked to quote poetry; Shakespeare, Longfellow, John Greenleaf Whittier, and James Whitcomb Riley; slogans, famous last words, scraps of wisdom from reliable sources—George Washington, Teddy Roosevelt, Ben Franklin's *Almanack*. We liked especially one lively version. You know how it goes:

> *For want of a nail the shoe was lost.*
> *For want of a shoe the horse was lost.*
> *For want of a horse the rider was lost.*

But he never stopped there. He went on. And on. A roaring voice, a rousing rhythm, his brows rollicking, carousing, his eyes razzle-dazzle, as when he teased us:

> *The battle was lost.*
> *The war was lost.*
> *The country was lost.*
> *The cause was lost.*

My sister and I listened with thralled faces. (One of the reasons we were so crazy about him—naturally, we were crazy about him—one of the reasons, strange to say, was that he was no disciplinarian. He gave us our lickings once a week, almost without fail; but he would never have thought to tell us to wash or eat or go to bed.) After all the hoarseness, the shouting, the excitement of battle, his voice would drop to a rumble—all the way to the basement. It came up through the floor, the soles of your feet:

The cause! The cause!

(We had no idea what a *cause* was.)

And all . . .

For want . . .

Of a nail.

It would be nice to be able to report that my mother's accusations were unfair; that I had been struck dumb from depth of emotion, sympathy for my father, fear for his injuries. But no one would fall for that, either. The fact is, it had never even crossed my mind that my father could hurt himself. Let alone that anyone else could. Let alone that I could. It never even crossed my mind that he could ask—want—need my sympathy.

"You go to your father," my mother said. "Right now. Right this minute. You march in there and you tell him. Say you're sorry you didn't say you're sorry."

There was a diagonal wriggling thing on the inside of his forearm—a fat shiny pink scar-worm—from his wrist halfway to his elbow, for years and years. For all I know it's there still.

A<small>ll night it rained.</small>

A newsreel rain; so I saw it in my sleep. Rain slashing through the dark, slanting against the windows, lashing the glass like the shackled leaves of the palm trees. Rain hosing down red tile and pink stucco and wrought-iron balconies; capsizing boats; swatting shutters; sousing trailer camps and truck farms and ten thousand lonely gas pumps. The palms and palmettos were kneeling in rain. Everything turned inside out—even the waves.

The morning was dark; the sky low and gray, the streets sleek and streaked with light. It took me a min-ute or two to realize they were flooded, the parked cars covered to hubcaps and bumpers. The neighbors were standing out on porches and stairs, squinting at the sky —helicopters flying low, props beating. The air was thick with sound. They were boats out fishing.

On the first floor all was activity; dragging out soggy swollen carpets, putting out chairs to dry. A car was coming through, slowly nudging sluggish water. Every-one clapped. It got slower and slower and chugged to a stop in the middle of the street. The driver got out, holding his jacket up over his head—pants rolled to his knees, legs eddies of hair—and ran off, plinking and plunking and hiding himself, like a mobster or convicted public official ducking the newsreel cameras.

The palm trees swayed, waving sliced streamers, tattered banners. Each and every leaf—notch—blade—was dripping light-sap. Tipped with pods of light.

There was some discussion of the relative advantages of first floors and second floors.

On the first floor you get more dampness, more bugs, more noise, and—as you see—you can expect now and then a little excitement. On the second floor, you can't use the screen porch as an outside entrance, and it might be a little hotter: it is believed that the Builders skimped on the roofing insulation. (It is believed that Builders skimp where they can, wherever you can't see, wherever they think they can get away with it. That is the nature of builders. Especially in South Florida.)

In spite of that, it is clear that the second floor would have the advantage over the first, but for one thing. It's the second floor. You have to walk up. That's fine for now. But for *how long?*

Builders in South Florida are like God in the universe. Their handiwork is everywhere, but they are nowhere to be seen. They move on, leaving Gardens of Eden all over the place, and nothing quite finished.

It was hard to tell if it was still raining or not; the smooth water stirring, ever so slightly, as if something might be blowing on it—a breath peck-pecking. The sun had disappeared; favors withdrawn. The helicopters kept passing through misty swamp. They had discovered another leak in the roof, another defect in the plans.

. . .

This development is now five years old; the ones who have been here that long are old-timers. It started out as a row of single-story, white-stuccoed duplexes. They were prefabs, and must have seemed pretty bare to begin with. I wouldn't be surprised if—in spite of wear and tear, water stains, dry rot, mildew—they look better now. Because now they are drenched in green; bunches and clusters of thick subtropical vegetation; names like sea grape, cocoplum, gumbo-limbo, nicker bean. (I've been reading the botanical labels on the nature trails again. Strange bedfellows.)

And there is plenty of space. They are on the canals, which are everywhere in South Florida; from muddy ditches, humble fishing holes—hardly enough for an alligator to wallow in, if that's what alligators do—to the Intracoastals, wide enough for drawbridges and seagoing vessels. People drive their golf balls into them and sometimes their cars.

But that was before the Boom. The new developers (the first had gone broke and everyone seems to think it serves them right) put up two-story structures; now there were four to each unit. And they built them closer. Pretty soon they weren't prefabs anymore; but they kept getting closer. They didn't face canals, either; they faced each other; over archways, walkways, stairways; and there was less and less space in between for anything green. Crimson hibiscus; spiky Spanish bayonet; the feathery shafts of the coconut palm.

Now you pay extra for a view. —The golf course, with its mounds and flags and thistled grass; or the distant stands of gray-green scrub oak and pine. The scrawny scruffy forest primeval of Florida. They look as if they might have been trees once, but they all drowned and died and these are their ghosts.

Still, the crows seem to think they are trees.

Someone will buy them and chop them down too.

The sections have names like Seville, Tuscany, Isle of Capri. Each condo has a letter; each apartment a number. So small wonder, what with fourteen thousand people living here, if visitors have a hard time finding their way. Everyone has stories of would-be guests who drive through the gates, past the guards in their kiosks, into the midst of all the look-alike buildings, parked cars, gridded streets, white lines, yellow stanchions; shiny brown Dempster Dumpsters on each and every corner. And pretty soon they get lost: they give up: they go home. Maybe they call the next day to apologize.

Everybody laughs at such tales. They know what it looks like: like every other development. Construction is everywhere, spreading westward, from the ocean, from the Intracoastals, from the Interstate; the setting sun winks and shimmers in the empty eyeholes of new buildings. —White. That is the color of Florida. In spite of the blue of ocean and sky and the living green of practically everything else. The white of limestone and fossilized seashell; that's what the whole state is made of, and that's what it's built of. Dug up; crushed for lime and cement; for roads and bridges and sparkling white high-rises. Also the color of clouds and golf balls and concave sails and gulls' gliding wings; of pretty white yachts leaving pretty white wakes. And Florida is so flat; it seems intentional. God must have meant it for condominiums. All those raw roofs rising instead of spooky trees; almost, like them, a mirage—the white dust scarcely settled. And all those billboards, promising that The Best Is Yet to Be.

And so? So what! This is Florida.

What could be easier than to heal this landscape; repair the breach, the damage and disruption, cranes, bulldozers, quick construction, transplanted populations. The flora down here is nothing like what you know up North; shy crocuses, shrinking violets, all those tendrils so bashfully wrapped up in themselves, peeping from leaves. These are tropical plants; they know how to compete. They shriek green; they screech it. You can see they belong to a more primitive age—when reptiles flew; pterodactyl plants, ridged and spiny, still can't make up their minds whether to wear feathers or fins. And none of your pale bulbs, either, that never see the light of day, and roots reaching deeply, secretively underground. In Florida, plants carry their roots with them; whole forests crawling on their bellies, recumbent trunks with roots that noose and lasso. They have claws, tusks, fangs, beaks. They can take anchor anywhere—the shallowest places; an inch or two of soil; on water; on other plants; on nothing at all—on air. The Spanish moss that beards the scenery—all those hanks of gray hair hanging like scalps from arthritic trees—that's an air plant. And so is that thing that might be the greasy-green cluster on top of a pineapple; it favors and festoons the gawky cypress. And what about the mangrove? Its roots grow up, not down; creep, crawl, grope, feel, latching on to whatever happens to come along—treasure troves of drift and debris. What the strangler fig does you might guess. And the banyan—the beautiful beautiful banyan (said to be the tree under which the Buddha found enlightenment, and why not?)—the banyan, with its tiers of leaves, puts down roots like trunks: porticoes: a veranda-tree, spreading green dominions. Looped, coiled, draped and doubled in roots—rope-roots—enough to hang itself, or to let down a ladder from heaven.

But the palm, the palm, is the original prefab plant. Height means nothing; even the roots of the royal palm are a handful, a bunch—as if you had yanked up some grass by the scruff of the neck. All you have to do is dig a hole or stick it in a pot, and aim a colored spotlight on it.

It's not true, what people say, about the toilets and the telephones. You can hear the phones ringing, sure, if the windows are open; and if the speaker happens to be a woman—the gravelly abrasive mannish voice some women get as they grow older (sea gulls on Social Security?)—yeah; you can hear that too. But you don't hear the plumbing. Absolutely not. That's a lie.

I'll tell you what you do hear. You hear everyone getting up in the middle of the night. Everyone has to, at least once.

Maybe you hear creaking: footsteps. A thud: the seat going up. Silence. Then you wait. A drip . . . a drop . . . an experimental dribble. More silence. Hey, you! You up there! What happened? What are you waiting for? Did you fall back asleep? Do you have to, or don't you? Are you going to do something and get it over with, or are you just going to stand there and think about it? Ah. That's right. That's better. That's more like it. —Did you get out of bed for nothing?

What's public about that? What could be more private? People minding their own business? We have heard the chimes at midnight.

The guards in the kiosks with their caps and their badges, waving you on with their clipboards, are a necessity, yes. People here are from the urban North; lower-middle, middle-middle-class Jews, Italians, Poles, other so-called ethnics—and they know all about it. That's the way we live now. In the older retirement areas, down in Miami, built before the days of guards and gates, the residents are sitting ducks. They may as well be on a Game Preserve. They are attacked—as the old are everywhere—with a ferocity that suggests other intentions; a kind of desecration; a destruction of our symbols (no matter how decrepit).

Nowhere are there more old people than in South Florida. And nowhere is the contrast greater, between youth and age. It's instructive to watch the aged, sitting on benches at the beach, watching the youth go by. They come down for spring vacation with surfboards under their arms—chained, fettered to them. So tall, so tan, so firm of flesh, so sound of limb, so white and solid of tooth and bone. Their sun-bleached, moon-blanched, wheaty-blond hair; their eyes as blue as their cut-off jeans. Meanwhile, here sit all the old ladies with freckled arms and wattled elbows and lavender hair that looks, I swear, as if they get it done in funeral parlors. And all the old gents lined up, with their hooked backs, their shoulders squatting at their ears. All the plastic teeth, the pink rinds for gums, the glasses so thick they give a vindictive sparkle. Pelicans perched on the shore —scythey necks sunk into their feathers, beaks buried in their breasts.

The waves roll in in generations, heaping up entangled sea life. Oozy weeds, unmolded jellyfish, driftwood and pickle jars toothed with barnacles, the deflated balloons—blue bubbles, on strings—of the man-of-war. Also: Styrofoam buoys, hairy coconut noggins, Frisbees, light bulbs, bottles, gym shoes. Bottles I can understand (how come no notes in them?), and maybe gym shoes; but light bulbs? Why light bulbs?

The air is bright, particulate; the glint and grit of white sand. The gulls flap up, spilling wings—scraps of light—glittering currents. The sky scatters blessings.

You have to understand. It's not just that the climate is nice, the weather sunny and warm—blue-skied, cloud-scudded. It's the air: it floats. One sniff and you're grateful. It smells of orange groves and salt water and, best of all, earth; pungent and potent as under the glass roofs of greenhouses. It's not just balmy: it is balm. Healing. A restorative. Heart's ease. Help for pain.

Who can blame them? Who would want to leave this? We get it all wrong. Beauty is here to stay. Beauty doesn't vanish. We do.

The guards at this development tend to be older than the residents. That is a fact. My father gave a lift to one who—taking off his cap and rubbing the nap of his thick white hair first this way and then that—owned up to eighty-six. He said he was getting "sick and tired of retirement." Since then my father has been consider-

ing: What to do in case of emergency? What if violence
should threaten? What if there should be an attack? —
How will he, my father—protect these poor old souls—
the guards—and come to their rescue?

The guards in the kiosks are a necessity, maybe; but
first and foremost, they are symbolic. Everybody knows
it. The residents themselves call all this "the Reserva-
tion." This is the line of demarcation, the border. —
"How long are you here for?" "What's the weather
doing back there?" That's what they all want to know.
Because it's nothing down here; that's not what they're
keeping out. It's what's back there; what they have left
behind them.

More than dirt, crime, crowding, corruption; more
than hard winters, blithering snows, icy streets; cars
that won't start, sidewalks that need shoveling. It's a
notion of life. Something they want to forget. Something bleak and somber they have traded in for things
undreamt of in their philosophy.

It's the Future.

All their lives they believed in the Future; they struggled and slaved and sacrificed for the Future. Not that
they had much choice; it was understood they had been
born too soon. Things were going to get better. In the
Future. The everlasting Future. And now all of a sudden they see the truth. The Future? What Future?
What's everybody talking about? Is there even going to
be such a thing? For the first time in their lives—for this
once and once only—it's an advantage to have been
born too soon. They won't have to stick around for the
Future. They leave it to us. See how we like it. Right
here, right now, right inside these gates—this thin line
of trees—they have just as much of the Future as they

want. They have caught up at last with American life, and they are going no farther.

The Future stops here.

Enough is enough.

My mother was on the telephone saying something about a flood. In her shortie nightgown, shoulders lifted, shrugging—the better to keep the thin straps up—her back a pair of brown water wings. Petals of white hair were clipped to her cheeks. She put her hand in front of her mouth when she saw me coming. A reflex, an instinct; she can't help it; she hides her mouth when her teeth are out.

It makes her look timid, flinching; someone stifling a scream, warding off a blow.

"It's true. I mean it. It's not just here. It's not just us. It's everyone. Everywhere. No one can get anywhere today. —I don't think he believes me," she said to me, talking behind her hand. "Right away he blames me. He thinks there's something the matter with the car."

This is something new, so I guess the teeth must be too. A complete upper plate? When did this happen? Her lip is pinched, puckered; she is trying to hold a bunch of pins in her mouth.

That's the way she talks; lips mincing, afraid to move; afraid she'll lose all her pins.

"What? The doctor was there? Well, good for him. — Can I help it if the doctor was there? Maybe there's no flood where he is. Maybe he came in a boat. He can afford it, I'm sure. —He said what? Back already? So soon? Oh, it was? Oh, it was. Oh. It was."

She held out the phone, her hand to her mouth, pumping up her little scarified eyebrows, biting down on her pins. Her hand is large and bumpy. She wears knuckles; other women wear rings.

"'S all right. 'S all right."

A deep basement grunt. The old repercussions.

Don't keep saying it's all right. It's not all right. We want to be with you.

"Take your time," he told me.

My mother hides her mouth; I don't know where she hides her teeth. Haven't seen anything pink and white blooming in water glasses. Maybe she keeps them under her pillow? —She hides her mouth even when she sleeps. On her back, the covers pulled to her nose, her hands—pawlike—gripping the sheets. I don't call this vanity. It's not the ugliness of old age she wants to keep to herself, it's the affliction. There is such a thing as self-defense.

I didn't mean to pry, but I saw. I saw, anyway. I looked in while she was sleeping. The covers had slipped down, her mouth had slipped open; sagged to one side—ajar—the way it does when she sleeps. Someone had let the air out of her. It's funny, you don't realize how much of a face is mouth: the armature, the support. It was the rest of her face that had collapsed; almost her whole face was mouth—the dreadful minced lips. It looked big, bigger than ever.

It looked like an exit.

"I *told* you not to say anything," she said to me. "I *told* you not to. Who asked you to?"

Her eyes are light brown, a yellowish tinge. Now that her skin is so tan, they are the same color as her face. The part—behind her hand—that is illuminated, moving.

I get a funny feeling in my parents' new home. Everything is new. Carpets, drapes, lamps; sofas with arms for cozying up to, cushions to get chummy with. A glass-topped coffee table with edges green as ice. There is even a china cabinet, shelves for displaying knickknacks (what folks down here call "momentos"). But where did it all come from? That is the question. Your guess is as good as mine.

People "redo" when they move to Florida; that's part of the ritual. I thought at first there were no cemeteries in the state; there are, you don't see them. They look like the farm fields they were just the other day; still standing, right next to them, surrounding them, without fences, the crops planted in parallel rows. (The cemetery gates, with their "Green"-this and "Garden"-that, pass easily for the promise of new developments.) Instead, you see warehouses; blocks of them, window-less white boxes. Some people bring all their worldly possessions—according to my mother—all that "dark ugly old furniture," all their "dark heavy winter clothes." And then: "Who needs it?" They put it all in these warehouses, and store it—as she says—"forever."

So I feel the way I might if I didn't know the people who live here. Not sure where to sit, what to touch. I walk around seeking what is familiar to me. The pots and pans, heavy hammered aluminum (they never looked new, so they don't look old); the portable TV (a suitable "momento," it does nothing but snow). Pictures of weddings and graduations. The decanter has a gold star pattern; it must be from Israel, where my sister lives now. (She'll be back; she moves around as much as I do.) Maybe those demitasse cups were housewarming gifts, like—I'm sure—the two bottles of Sabra they put out when company comes, and put back when company leaves.

I keep looking at the china cabinet. Candlesticks, candy dishes, figurines; things that rattle and chink and catch the light. I look so much, I make them nervous. Shelves tremble, glass shivers; ceramic eyes *shine:*

—Psst. Watch out. Knock it off. Here she comes again.

—What? Her? Oh no, not again. What's she up to, anyhow?

—She wants to see if we're worth anything, dope.

—Well I like that! Of all the nerve.

So that's the way it is? That's a fine how-do-you-do. My parents are getting on in years, they're living in a Retirement Village. My father is lying right this moment in a hospital bed—they just took out half his gut; my mother is napping on the couch, hands nailed together atop her breast, a mouth like a punctured tire. The Last Act. —And I'm inspecting their possessions? Looking it all over, to see how I like it?

So that's the kind of person I am.

That's nice to know.

All of a sudden, it came to me: My parents have never had *things* before.

Not like other people have; not like everybody else;

possessions, acquisitions, matters of taste—choice—
pleasure—pride. Considerations of a sort which rarely
entered our lives. No wonder all this is new to me; no
wonder it's such a strange sensation. I'm not used to
looking upon their belongings as anything of value, sentimental or otherwise. But especially sentimental. The
luster of associations, of memories. As anything to be
kept; worth keeping; to be passed on; potentially mine.
Keepsakes.

Someday, in the ordinary course of events, it will fall
to my lot to get rid of all this. And what am I supposed
to do with it then? Will someone please tell me? Where
can I put it? How can I keep it? I have no place of my
own. I've been storing belongings in this one's basement, that one's attic, for years. And I don't want to get
rid of it; separate it; any of it. I want it all just as it is,
every last bit. Intact.

This is the scene of their happiness.

Maybe I can rent a warehouse?

What funny people. My parents. Still don't understand my sister and me. How come we live the way we
do. Why we don't "have anything"; never seem to settle
down. (Why can't we be like other people's children,
acquiring things, habits for a lifetime?) The same way
they can't understand why and how come we never
learned to speak Yiddish.

Our grandparents spoke a crude and broken English,
and we thought that other language they spoke—harsh,
guttural to us—was crude and broken too. Our parents
spoke Yiddish for privacy's sake. How else could they
conduct this grim business of their grownup lives? They

talked *about* us in Yiddish, all the time; but never *to* us.
—Sitting at the table in morning darkness, my father
dragging dragging the spoon in his coffee. (He was
awfully fond of sugar; kept heaping it in until there was
nothing left in his cup but silt—sludge—glittering
sand.) Oh, we knew what they were saying all right.
Someone had got sick, or died. Someone had lost
money, or a job. Someone had done something wrong
—though she didn't know what; and was going to get
a licking—though she wouldn't know why.

Like oars thick in weeds, the sound of their voices
slapped in our ears, got tangled in sleep.

They had learned Yiddish at home; their first language, the primary language, the expression of feeling
and family life. For them it meant a separation between
that life and the rest. (What they called "this cockeyed
world.") But for us it meant a division within the family
itself; barriers between parents and children; bitterness
fated; something banished and denied.

And yet I knew all along that Yiddish was the primary
language, an original tongue. All other speech would
never be more than a polite translation. This was the
Source. Things were named by their rightful names,
names that could hurt; given their true weight and
force. Nothing could be taken back. It was all Last
Words.

My mother, for all she looks like a stabbing victim,
keeled over on the couch, is making purring noises,
humming to herself, her motor left running. She does
that now, both sleeping and waking. If this is old age,
she sounds contented with it. And I forgot to say: we

took off our shoes when we came in the door.

That's family for you. Right back where I started:

There is nothing here I would ever choose—and nothing I can ever part with.

S o. Here we go again. The distant, the steadfast, the enduring. My father's stern and rock-bound features. Elevated. Snoring. His head is huge—precipitous. Steep-banked brow. Broken nose. Quarried cheeks. The skin not so much pocked and pitted as granular, eroded; the mica flash of whiskers beneath.

A pile of sandstone on a high white pillow.

His lips are smooth in his rough face.

My father's snoring is an old scenario. Action-packed adventure. Good guys vs. bad guys. Hair-raising rescues and narrow escapes. Storms at sea; sword duels; catapults and cannon. All this and more, courtesy of *Liberty Comics*—*Wonder Woman, Batman & Robin,* and *The League of Justice;* James Fenimore Cooper and Victor Hugo in *Classic Comics* editions; fairy tales dramatized over Saturday-morning radio to sound effects that whistled and swooned; and mealy-papered, close-printed library books that began with dashes—and took my breath away: "One day in the year 177–, in the village of M—"

My father was David *and* Goliath; Samson *and* the Philistines; Jack *and* the Giant. Daniel and the whole damn den.

And to think he had been such a puny kid.

At the time of his Bar Mitzvah, almost fourteen, he was still the shortest one in his class. He posed for his photo in cap, knickers, prayer shawl, some tome open on the lectern table beside him; and you can see how he has to hoist his elbow and hitch it up in order to lean against the table. The face is already his face; a mug, a muzzle, a kisser. It's as if he had stuck his head through a hole in a cardboard poster, like those trick shots you take at carnivals and amusement parks.

He sprouted, in the proverbial manner, overnight. It took the rest of him a while to catch up. At the time of his marriage, ten years later, he weighed one hundred eighty-five pounds and looked gaunt. Starved. The heavy-boned, hollowed cheeks, the lumpy throat and cliffy brow of the young Abe Lincoln. There are props in this one too; his white bow tie, the white carnation in his buttonhole, the stiff paper cone of his bride's bouquet and the swirling train of her veil (a curtain someone swiped off a window)—all belong to the studio. Like the backdrop they are standing in front of; a waterfall, a stream, frothy bushes, frills of trees. —After this is over, after the click, after he yanks his head out of the box, the photographer is going to take it all back, put it away.

It was the stock story, told in all those comic books. *Superman, Captain Marvel* (there was a Marvel family, and I'm not sure but what there may have been a Marvel dog), and all the rest, had ordinary everyday identities; but when they tore off their shirts, or their specs, or shouted out the magic word *(Shazam!),* they became their true selves—hero selves—and invincible. A story retold in the smudgy back pages as well. Those ads featuring the famous "97 lb. weakling," in his roomy bathing shorts, with legs like white worms, and two little —oh pitifully little!—dots on his chest. On the beach he is mocked by bullies; they laugh at him and kick sand in his face and on his blanket. He sends for the *Charles Atlas Course;* and the next time those wise guys show up, are they in for a surprise. A real shocker.

There would be a photo (actual) of Charles Atlas himself; legs solid in skimpy trunks, chest massy, head bowed; looking unmistakably like my father—something grim-lipped, stoical in this self-made strength. What had worked for him could work for you.

Mind Over Matter.

There was a moral to these stories. Is there anyone in the world who doesn't know it by heart? All those pip-squeaking, four-eyed, timorous alter egos; all those heroes who could fly through the air and laugh at bullets. Escape! Escape from this weak and helpless condition of childhood! Growing up was growing invulnerable. That's what we thought.

My father used to emerge from these struggles victorious. Now it seems from the rattles and sighs and phlegm catching in his throat—those two noisy excavations, his nostrils—that he might be getting the worst of it; taking his lumps. I hear blows.

The room overlooked the entrance to the hospital— three or four stories high, pink stucco sticking up for miles around. The usual landscaping outside the glass doors: grass laid down in patches—squares—rough green toupees; spindly, scantily clad palms bending and bowing in colored spotlights. These were buttressed with poles as thin as they were. And the usual digging:

a new wing being added, the parking lot expanded, mounds and pits all over the place. Today the holes were water and clay. The roads were still slimy with mud, the grass and fields blubbering with it. Everywhere, stranded tractors, bulldozers, trailers, and the rusty beat-up pickup trucks of migrant workers. —The green peppers stood row on row, polished to ripeness. But the bosses weren't taking any chances on sending their equipment out into all that muck; they were afraid of ruining their machinery. They walked up and down in squelching boots, talking here and there to angry pickers. Most of the pickers weren't talking to anybody; not even to each other. They sprawled on the trucks. Some of them seemed to be wet—soaked to the skin— as if they had spent the night out in the rain. It was their stocking hats and processed hair, stuck to their heads like large wet leaves.

All along the roads lay frayed flattened shoelaces that turned out to be dead snakes. Hundreds of dead snakes, and pale pink blood-prints.

My father quarrelled with his mother. Never mind the whole story—because what's the whole story?—but anyone would have said he was in the right. For all the good. And shouldn't he—of all people—have known better? Who was it who was forever telling me? Might Made Right. Two Wrongs Didn't. Sleeping Dogs Lied.

He had been the dutiful son; he had *shown respect.* (One of the truly mystical phrases of my childhood. I couldn't figure out what it meant. I had never *seen* any *respect.*) It was the first and only time he ever stood up to her. How was he supposed to know she would make so much of it? Backs turned, doors slammed, telephones banged down, letters sent back in shreds. — How was he to know she would die suddenly, one foot on the floor, trying to get out of bed?

The phone call. The rush to the house. The trucks standing outside. A long red fire truck, a hook-and-ladder, motor running—shuddering—pumping noise by the gallon. The street seemed flooded and dammed.

It was a stone-faced two-flat with a brief front lawn and all the doors and windows were open. My father ran up the steps. A fireman in shovel helmet and hip boots was coming out backwards, an ax at his belt, carrying one end of something. Black rubber or oilcloth, same as his slicker. Two men were holding up the other end and shouting directions at him:

Keep Going Watch Out Easy Does It Keep Going

He glanced over his shoulder, bumping down the stairs.

His boots sank in soft mud and sprinkled grass seed.

The next morning I heard my father getting up. He always rose mute, with a mouthful of phlegm, and headed straight for the bathroom—holding up his pants, holding out his lip—looking neither left nor right until he'd had a chance to spit. I heard the floors resounding under his heavy bare feet, then the hoarse rash noise. First thing he always did.

That had been the hardest blow of his life. He told me so himself. (Sometimes he forgets when he's talking to me and when he's not, and who wouldn't get confused, after all these years?) Why he would want to pass on such pain; why he should be so bound and determined to inflict this bitterness, I can't say. But we have to pass on something, don't we? Otherwise, what's the good? What are children for?

A plastic bag, hooked to a plastic tube, was slowly slowly seeping light-sap, one clear liquid bead leaked at a time. Another, larger bag, clipped to the side of the bed, was sudsing and slushing. The arms over the covers hairy and sunburnt; a circle of sunburnt skin round the neck. A sprinkle of grizzled hairs—singed, frizzed—they'd crumble if you touched them. The width, the depth of the chest—the coarse sheet-blanket stretched across it—seems pretty much what it has always been; the forearms still viny with tendon and vein. But the upper arms and shoulders don't bear the load they used to, don't pull their own weight. They seem to slope and slump from the humped muscles of the neck.

The hair is cocoon white, and of that texture. It looks frivolous above porous yellow earthworks.

An eyebrow tugs.

A lid lifts.

I see blue.

"Oh, Sal. Well well well. Look who's here. 'Lo, Sal." An iron door scraping on its hinges. "So you made it, I see? So you got here all right? Everything all right, then?"

"Fine fine. How about you?"

"This? This is nothing. A Rough Customer, that's all."

"Which do you mean? It or you?"

"Oh-oh. My daughter's here. She's ribbing me. She's giving me the business."

Still looking at me out of one eye. Still whispering—lip stiff, as if he has to spit.

"And your mother? Where's she at?"

"She's coming. Don't worry." A little trouble with the car. I'm not supposed to mention, among other things, cars and floods.

There is a deep deep dent over the bridge of his nose, right between the eyes. From the accident, still? Or is this from his glasses? We're used to them by now; so used to them, we forget. We think it's the lenses that make his eyes so blue—blinking—on the brink. The truth of the matter is, the new nose is an improvement over the old one; not so roughhewn. High-crested, flattened at the tip. Abrupt. Abutting. If you'll pardon the expression, a real butte.

I put my hand on the middle of his forehead. The middle of his forehead is the size of my hand; a saddle, a slope. The heavy ridge over each brow smoothed as with the stroke of a thumb.

I see what it is. I see what it is. With my mother age is a disguise; she puts it on with a wink. (Some wink.) But with my father it is another matter altogether. Age is revealing him; the essential in him; completing the job. It scares me. Hacked, chipped, chiselled, gouged. The mark of the craftsman's hand, the craftsman's tools.

In his mortared face the niche of blue eye is like a glimpse of the sky in whiskered stone walls; monuments or ruins.

He doesn't mean it.

This hurts him more than it hurts you.

You know he really loves you.

He's *still* your father!

Who would have thought? That all those things my mother says would turn out to be true?

This is the way my father shows his love.

What's more. What's more. This is the way he feels it.

I saw her coming, in flats and slacks, arms swinging at her sides, white head moving briskly along with the rhythm. Florida white. White as gulls' wings. Turning out her feet smartly, the way she does; such conviction in her step I could see the soles of shoes.

Whaddayaknow. Taps on her toes.

And she shall have music wherever she goes.

I opened the vent. "Here she comes now."

Very distinctly the taps could be heard, singing out on the sidewalk—announcing and identifying her. Arms, legs, shoulders, flat brown cheeks, Indian-head nickel nose—all of her seemed to be pointing one way, heading in the right direction.

My father must have heard the sound, familiar enough to him; and it must have brought to mind what I was seeing. And a whole lot more. Because he shut his eyes and laughed to himself, his chin and his voice in his chest, his thick forehead bunched in a frown—as if it hurt him some, all the same.

"'S her all right. Know her anywhere."

The glass doors glided open; she glided through.

Puddles were beginning to gleam in the parking lot. In the colored spotlights the palm trees bent their bundled sheaves. Over the chilled dried racketing of the air conditioner the night air was coming in: mammal warm. You could all but catch it and keep it.

I put out my hand. I shut my eyes too.

Yes. Please. Give them ten years.

A NOTE ON THE TYPE

This book was set, via computer-driven
cathode-ray tube, in a film version of a
typeface called Baskerville. The face itself
is a facsimile reproduction of types cast
from molds made for John Baskerville
(1706–75) from his designs. Baskerville's
original face was one of the forerunners
of the type style known as "modern face"
to printers—a "modern" of the period
A.D. 1800.

Composed, printed and bound by
The Haddon Craftsmen, Inc.,
Scranton, Pennsylvania

Book design by Judith Henry